Arlene Johnston

Jule's Story

Pine Lake Books
West Guilford

© 2010 Arlene Johnston

All rights reserved. No part of this book may be reproduced, stored in a retrieval system or transmitted in any form or by any means without the prior written permission of the publishers, except by a reviewer who may quote brief passages in a review to be printed in a newspaper, magazine or journal.

First printing

Pine Lake Books has allowed this work to remain as the author intended.

All characters in this book are fictitious, and any resemblance to real persons, living or dead, is coincidental.

Library and Archives Canada Cataloguing in Publication

Johnston, Arlene, 1951-
    Jule's story / Arlene Johnston.

Issued also in an electronic format.
ISBN 978-0-9813539-6-8

    I. Title.

PS8619.O4845J85 2010   jC813'.6   C2010-904003-1

ISBN: 978-0-9813539-6-8

West Guilford
www.pinelakebooks.webs.com
pinelakebooks@gmail.com

DEDICATION

To Jule Albert,
my teacher, my inspiration, my love.

ACKNOWLEDGEMENTS

Lynn Simpson, my editor and publisher. Thank you for your patience and great editing skills.

Other Books by Pine Lake Books

Final Justice by L.M. Henderson
Ryan Arthur, Knight by Lynn Henderson
Blood Connection by Lynn Marie Simpson

Coming Soon
Rocket and the Tadpoles by Lynn Henderson
Bellus Terra by Tammy Woodrow
Sunny Honeybee is Lost by Tammy Woodrow
Lorah's Promise by Ann Harris

1

JULE OPENED HIS right eye catching a glimpse of morning sunshine as the curtain blew open before a hefty wind gust sucked it back toward the dusty screen. He turned onto his back and listened to the loose trill of a male eastern phoebe serenading its mate. Once again, the gray-brown, sparrow-sized birds had built their nest on top of the curved green metal hose holder, bolted to the side of the house, hidden safely under the deck. It was the perfect set up. Not only could the birds gain entry through the crisscross lattice work in front, but there was also an exit through the diamond shaped lattice at the far end of the wooden deck. Everyone was fine with this arrangement, except Dad, who was already complaining about the hose lying all over the grass for the third year in a row.

Jule glanced at the bright red numbers on the clock radio beside his bed and watched as 7:59 turned to 8:00 a.m. *She's late. Nope. Here she comes.* He lay still listening as the approaching footsteps beat a steady rhythm on the puritan pine, stained wood floor that leads to his bedroom. He knew the routine very well. After all, it had been going on since he entered grade one.

"Good morning my sweet bird feeder," Mom called out, opening the bedroom door. "Time to get up for school," she said cheerfully, walking over to the window and drawing back the navy curtains. "It's a lovely spring day," she said, looking out the window. "Claire is waiting for you," she smiled before closing the bedroom door and walking back down the hallway.

Jule lay in bed mimicking his mother. She was his official timekeeper, weather announcer and curtain opener. He wanted to wake up with the clock radio alarm like his older sister, Kristen, who has been getting up on her own for years. He would have to have to talk to Mom about replacing her daily routine with the radio. He just wasn't sure when. He knew it would probably upset her. *Maybe today*, he decided sliding out of bed, stretching as he walked toward the window. He stood and watched as a black-capped, white-breasted nuthatch moved headfirst down the tree, searching for insects. *Lucky bird, no school for you.* He picked up his beige khaki shorts and forest green t-shirt off the floor beside his desk, then headed toward the bathroom.

Jule walked into the bright, sunny kitchen with its two large picture windows and noticed a bowl of granola cereal sitting on the place mat in front of the oak chair he sits in. Kristen's place mat was empty. *That's another thing I have to talk to Mom about, making my own breakfast choices.* "Here's your orange juice," she smiled, handing him a tall glass. *I wanted apple juice.* "Thanks Mom," he said, taking the glass. "Where's Kristen?" he asked, sitting down at the table. He already knew the answer. For the past three weeks, she had been taking much longer to get ready for school. Ever since that new kid transferred to Haliburton from Fenlon Falls a few weeks ago, she made sure she looked hot.

Jule's Story

"Getting ready for school. She's been up for over an hour," Mom replied.

Jule looked up from his cereal bowl, as the door to the kitchen swung wide open.

Mom commented on how pretty Kristen looked in her beige skinny jeans, blue paisley cotton shirt and stonewashed denim jacket.

Jule knew she would freak out, but couldn't resist this opportunity to bug her. "Probably has something to do with Adam Fullerton," he said, looking down at his cereal.

"Oh, shut up!"

"Kristen! Don't talk to your brother like that."

"He's such a jerk!"

"Kristen loves Adam."

"That's enough you two," Mom cut in. "Hurry now Jule or you'll miss the bus."

With two hands, he hoisted his cereal bowl and tipped its contents into his mouth, wiped his face with his hand, then grabbed the dark-brown backpack sitting on the floor beside him. He waited for his mom to scoop a handful of sunflower seeds from the blue plastic pail sitting by the door. Again, this was another routine of hers he could easily do himself.

"Aren't you working at Cindy's?" he asked, as she replaced the lid.

"No, not until Wednesday, I'll spend the day writing my novel. Love you to pieces."

"Love you too, Mom." Jule latched the screen door then began whistling and calling for Claire. She's around here somewhere he knew, shielding his eyes from the bright sunshine as he searched the surrounding trees.

He watched as she bounced her way through the air toward his outstretched handful of seeds, landing on his middle finger to select just the right one. Claire, a black-capped chickadee, he began feeding by hand months ago, visited his outstretched hand daily for sunflower seeds. As usual, it didn't take long before other chickadees joined her, landing on Jule's head, shoulders and arms awaiting their turn.

Kristen began her daily protest. Why did he have to do this every morning at the bus stop? "You are so weird and soon everyone will think that," she said, moving away from him and his flock of birds, as she tied back her long blond hair. Her friends were already calling him a geek.

"You should try it sometime, Sis. It's really neat connecting with nature." Jule rubbed his hands together, after Claire took the last seed.

"Well, I wish you would connect with nature somewhere else. You are soooo embarrassing me." She quickly boarded the mustard coloured school bus and sat up front with her friends, purposely not looking at her brother as he headed toward the back. Unlike most of the kids who wanted to sit and talk to their friends, Jule preferred sitting next to the window for the twenty minute ride to J. Douglas Hodgson School in the town of Haliburton. From this vantage point, he spent the time observing the seasonal changes of the forests, lakes and rivers. Every day, there was something new to see. Today, a pair of loons were swimming around Jim Beef Lake trying to decide where they will build a nest to raise their young. Though each season has its own unique beauty, spring was his favourite time of year, when the forests would come back to life, as winter's snowy blanket retreated and melted into much needed moisture for the trees. This year, the new foliage seemed more vibrant than ever, with its bright shades of yellow-green and lime-green. He wished he was sitting on a rock by the river casting a fishing line. The bus was just passing his favourite rock face when someone tapped him on the shoulder, distracting him.

"Is this seat taken?"

Jule turned toward the inquisitive green-eyed girl with tightly-braided dark brown hair hanging over her right shoulder like a large brown snake. It reminded him of the huge water snakes that would hang themselves out to dry on sunny days, wrapped around tree branches that jutted out over the river. *Ah! Stop the bus! It's been invaded by the snake girl! Get a big net! Contain the beast! Slip it over her head and scoop her in, snake and all.* "No," he replied, turning back to the window wondering what happened to the snakes that they often mistook for tree branches.

"My name is Natalie," she continued, sitting down next to him. "What's your name?"

The snake girl has a name. I wonder what she calls her snake. Betty? Lizanne? Kristen? That's it. Kristen. "Jule," he said, staring out the window wishing the girl and her snake would slither back to where they came from.

"Jule," she said, with a slight accent. "It's French, isn't it?"

"Yup." *At least she didn't make fun of it.*

"I see you feeding those sweet little birds at the bus stop every morning. What are they?"

"Black-capped chickadees," he said, continuing to stare out the window. *We are almost at the school. Why doesn't she get the hint that I don't want her or her stupid snake anywhere near me?*

"I think that is so neat. I wish I could do that."

Hmm. A smart snake girl. Not many of them around. "You can," he said, turning to face her. "All you need are some sunflower seeds and a little patience, then you will have them eating right out of your hand." *Better get rid of the snake though. Chickadees aren't keen on hanging reptiles.*

The bus slowed to a stop in front of the school. "I can hardly wait to try feeding them. Thanks for telling me how to get chickadees to eat out of my hand," Natalie smiled, getting up from the seat.

Jule remained seated and watched as Natalie and her snake, which now hung straight down the middle of her back, walk over to a group of girls. He was surprised at her interest in chickadee feeding. Kristen wouldn't be caught dead doing that! The bus driver turned around and stared at Jule who began moving quickly down the aisle. He bid the driver good day, jumped from the top step onto the sidewalk then ran quickly to the side entrance of the school.

The halls were filled with chattering kids making their way to their classrooms, as the 8:45 bell sounded to start classes. The teachers lined the hallway coaxing the kids along. It was too nice a day to be in school, so it took some extra convincing.

Jule's teacher, Ms. Annadale, waited at the classroom door and watched as the kids scrambled for their desks and began to settle down. "Let's try to get to our seats a little quieter and quicker next time," she said, as her eyes scanned the room for empty seats. "For today's writing assignment, I would like you to write about a special place you would like to visit. It could be in another country or a certain place you enjoy going to, such as Toronto or a friend's cottage. You may use the encyclopedias. And don't forget your dictionaries. I would like them handed in before recess, please. Let's get to work now."

Jule remained at his desk and watched as his classmates scrambled for the encyclopedias that lined three metal shelves near the front of the classroom, then reached into his desk for the dictionary and began flipping through the tattered pages. *I have my special place up here in my head*, he smiled, twirling his straight brown hair with a pencil, organizing his thoughts.

When the bell sounded for recess, the students handed in their stories before leaving the classroom. Jule handed his to the teacher. "You seem to enjoy writing," Ms. Annadale smiled.

"I do, a lot. Writing stories lets me go wherever my imagination transports me."

"I always look forward to reading your stories. You have such a vivid imagination."

He smiled and made a mental note to look up 'vivid' in the dictionary.

Jule walked out the side door of the school into the bright sunshine, raising his hand to shield the sun from his eyes, as he heard his name being called. It was Andrew Thompson yelling and waving frantically from centerfield. He stood motionless trying to decide whether he felt like playing baseball, especially without his glove. He wasn't sure where he had left it, then he remembered seeing it beside the clock radio this morning. He had left it there as a reminder to bring it to school. Andrew kept beckoning him to join the game. Finally, Jule ran quickly toward him.

"It's about time," he said, punching his glove. "We need another fielder."

Jule scanned the baseball diamond. The bases were loaded and there was one out, according to Andrew. Once again, Bozo Barrett had hand picked his team, making sure he got the best players every time or he wouldn't play. Now the short, stocky, blond haired, freckle-faced Barrett stood riveted to the chainlink fence that divided the benches from the playing field, coaxing Jamie Laking, the team's best batter, to not hold back and clobber the ball.

"Come on Laking! You can do it!" Barrett encouraged, as the pitch sailed over the plate and Laking swung missing it by a mile. *Idiot.* "Keep your eye on the ball!" he yelled tersely from the sidelines, as he felt the chainlink fence dig into his fleshy hands. *If we lose this game, I'll never hear the end of it.* Finally, Laking connected hard with the third pitch sending it flying high into the air. "Run!" Barrett screamed, letting go of the fence.

Andrew watched as the ball started descending back to earth with Jule running backward to retrieve it. The ball landed in his cupped hands with a hard smack. He then fired it into home where the catcher tagged the last runner.

"Nice catch!" Andrew said, patting him on the back as they made their way toward the bench. "And with no glove! You're up to bat first."

Jule walked over to the stack of bats lined up against the six-foot fencing and swung a couple of them until he found a metal bat that felt right.

"Well, well. If it isn't Julie," Barrett said, as Jule took his place at home plate. *I'll make toast of this little jerk.* "Keep your eye on the ball," he said sarcastically, before pitching a hard right.

"Strike one," their catcher yelled, as the ball flew over the plate.

"What's wrong Julie? Too fast for ya?" Barrett chuckled, getting ready for the next pitch.

Jule tightened his grip on the bat. Barrett may be a jerk, but he was one of the best pitchers in the school. He watched closely as Barrett tried to distract him with his constant banter before the next pitch. Ironically, he had thrown himself off with all his yapping and pitched another hard right that Jule anticipated. He swung with all his might and connected bat to ball with a loud twang, firing the ball like a burning meteorite into right field.

"That's a homer!" Andrew yelled, jumping up from the bench, as the ball whizzed quickly past the side of Barrett's head.

"Go Jule go!" his team chanted, as he rounded the bases heading toward home. "Nice hit!" his team congratulated him, as the bell sounded ending recess. Barrett was not impressed, as he began shoving through the team huddle with his teammates following close behind. He came to a halt a few centimeters in front of Jule. "You almost hit me in the head," Barrett said, running his hand over the left side of it, standing as tall as he could to meet Jule's gaze. Even standing on his toes, he was still a few centimeters shorter.

Too bad I missed Jule thought, as Barrett breathed his garlic breath all over him. "Gee Barrett, I'm really sorry," he said, holding back a gag. He was beginning to feel ill.

"Do you mean that?" Barrett asked, noting his sarcastic tone.

"Of course I do."

"I don't believe you."

"Then maybe you should settle with keeping your eyes on the ball. I believe that was your advice to Laking just a few minutes ago," Jule smiled, before walking away.

"You little grade four jerk. I can beat your butt anytime. Julie, Julie, Julie," Barrett chanted, as his team joined in.

Andrew caught up to Jule saying Barrett was the jerk, and thanked him for playing on his team.

Jule nodded then ran for the side door, as the chanting continued. He was unaware of the group of girls standing on the pavement watching him run inside the school. "There goes Jule," Natalie said, as they walked toward the entrance.

"I sat beside him on the bus this morning. He has the cutest dimpled smile, though he's not very talkative. But he did tell me how to feed chickadees right out of my hand."

"You're lucky he said that much," Cody said. "I've heard he's really quiet and likes to keep to himself."

"Well, I'm going to get to know him better," Natalie smiled.

At the end of the day, the kids began boarding the buses back home. Jule went to a seat at the back of the bus. Luckily, Natalie remained up front with her friends. The last thing he needed was some stupid girl yapping and interrupting his thoughts. He sat quietly by the window thinking of his fishing spot down by the river, until the bus pulled up in front of his house. He was first to disembark and ran in through the backdoor.

"How was your day?" Mom asked.

"Okay," he said, hanging his backpack up on a hook near the door.

"Anything new or exciting?"

"Nope. I'd much rather be fishing," he replied, cutting a piece of chocolate cake.

"I bet, considering he almost knocked Barrett out when he drove a baseball right at his head," Kristen said, coming in the back door.

Jule put down his piece of cake and turned toward Kristen. "You saw my homer?"

"No, but I heard all about it. Barrett is in my class, you know."

"Poor Barrett." Jule mumbled, reaching for a banana to eat with his cake. He was not surprised that Kristen, with her radar hearing, didn't miss his comment.

"You stupid bird feeding weirdo!"

"Kristen! That is no way to talk."

"He is so embarrassing, Mom. All the kids make fun of him."

"I hope you stick up for him. After all, he is your brother."

"Yeah, I am your brother," he sang out, as Kristen stormed out of the kitchen.

Exasperated, Mom watched as the kitchen door swung closed once again. "Do you have any homework?"

"Just a bit of math and reading," he said, finishing the last of his cake. "Can I go fishing?"

"Yes. Be home by six," she said, trying to kiss the top of his head as he ran by. He was getting so tall that soon she won't be able to reach it. Jule was growing up far too quickly for her liking. She felt like she was losing her baby. This wasn't the first time he had made a hasty exit to avoid her. He's probably anxious to fish, she concluded, heading to the stove to start supper.

Jule grabbed his fishing rod standing beside the back door and ran quickly down the tree-lined road until he spotted three large boulders covered in new lime-green moss. The boulders marked the beginning of a very worn pathway that led to the beaver pond. He ran further along until he came to a small ledge of slate grey rocks, situated a few meters back from the road, that were also coated with fresh springtime moss. This rock ledge marked the beginning of a hidden path leading to a quiet area, surrounded by huge ancient white pine trees. Breathless, Jule stood in the middle of this peaceful forest, gazing up at the majestic height of the evergreens, taking slow, deep breaths of pine-scented air. This was definitely his favourite time of year when everything came back to life again. He sat down on a large fallen ash tree resting against the rotting trunk of another and concluded, the pine trees rule. All the downed trees were either ash or maple. Trees that were here long before him.

He reached into his pocket for sunflower seeds then began whistling to attract the chickadees, waiting patiently for their response. Poor Natalie. He had forgotten to mention the whistling necessary to attract them quickly. She probably won't bother anyway, he concluded. Soon the area was alive with the tiny birds perching on his head, shoulders and arms waiting their turn at the seeds in his cupped hand. The tiny acrobats are so clever and friendly, as they circle and dive for seeds. He often spoke to them. "How was your day? Mine was okay, except for the school part. The classroom part is okay. It's just recess. The older kids are so mean to me when they call me Julie. The truth is, I wish my name was Brian or Doug. Anything but Jule. But you don't care what my name is. You like me no matter what. When I am with you, I feel really good. Too bad it couldn't always be like this." *It must be mating season.* The chickadees were becoming more aggressive, as they fought for the remaining seeds. He promised to bring them more tomorrow, as he picked up his old fishing rod and continued walking along a tree-lined path he had marked a few years ago with an old white shoe lace, now faded gray, tied to a sturdy maple tree branch. It was a survival tactic he learned at cub camp when his dad was a leader of the troop, before he got too busy at his new job. Jule was surprised to see the branch that the lace was tied to was at least 30 centimeters higher off the ground than last year. He no longer needed the marker to tell him which path to take because he knew this area very well. As he continued, he listened for the sound of the river that was easier to hear in the spring. The winter runoff and spring rains created a fast flowing, deeper current in most areas of the river. He stood at the edge watching the water cascade over the rocks and was amazed by how the noise and scenery still gave him goose bumps. He loved this area so much. Jule sat down on a large grey-black boulder near the river's edge and cast his line into a deep pocket of water. He turned skyward and watched as a large bird circled slowly in the cloudless sky. From where he sat, it was difficult to identify which bird of prey it was but narrowed it down to an eagle or osprey. He had spent many hours researching bird and wildlife habitat in this area and was pretty sure it was one or the other. He continued studying the bird and concluded it was an osprey because its wingtips were slightly angled. Whereas, an eagle's broad wings are flat during flight. He had seen this bird circling in the sky before, but never witnessed what happened next. The bird began to plummet straight down like it was going to crash into the river, stopping just short of it. With beating wings, it hovered a few seconds then plunged feet-first into the river, emerging with a large dripping fish in its talons, flying in front of him close to the water. Jule sat mesmerized, watching as the bird's powerful wings cut through the air, holding on tightly to what had to be a four-pound steelhead. Once it was out of sight further down the river, Jule gulped deep breaths of air to calm his racing heart. *That was amazing!* It was definitely an osprey. This raptor is easy to identify by the dark eye strip, extending over its bright yellow eyes, on an otherwise white crown and forehead. The breast and belly are white. The tail and wings are finely barred black and grey. Also, his research revealed that the osprey is the only raptor that plunges into the water, feet first.

Once his excitement subsided, he concluded the fish had to be at least a four-pound steelhead. It was getting close to supper time so he decided not to cast off again. He reeled in his line then slowly walked home, thinking about the osprey and the steelhead it held onto so tightly. *I wish I could catch one like that.*

At home, Jule washed up for dinner then went into the great room to see his father who sat quietly reading the paper.

"Hey Dad."

"Hey son. Mom tells me you've been fishing. Any luck?" he said, not looking up from the paper.

Jule stared at the picture on the front page of the *Echo* of a toddler being pushed by her dad. "No luck." He wanted to tell him about the osprey that scooped the fish but changed his mind, opting not to disturb him.

"You'll get one next time," he said, turning a page of the newspaper. "How was your day?"

Jule was surprised he had asked. *Maybe he isn't too occupied after all.* "Good, thanks. How was yours?" he said, settling back into the dark beige sofa ready to tell him about the osprey.

"Very busy," he said, closing the paper, looking toward him.

"You are always busy."

His dad stared at him like he was from another planet, then spoke. "That's what happens when you are all grown up and have to go to work. That's why it's important for you to enjoy your youth before you have to take on adult responsibilities."

If this is what adulthood was all about, Jule wanted no part of it. He sat and watched as his dad folded the *Echo* and walked toward the kitchen, and then reluctantly followed.

Mom handed the dinner plates to Kristen, who placed them on the brown place mats, then called everyone to the table. As his mom passed Jule the carrots, she mentioned that his teacher had called.

"Skipping school again," Kristen said, interrupting as usual.

Mom put down the bowl of mashed potatoes and looked in Kristen's direction. "He doesn't do that anymore. Ms. Annadale called to tell me what a good writer he is and how much she enjoys his stories."

"Sounds like a chip off the old block," Dad said, looking lovingly across the table at Mom.

"My teacher said I write good stories too," Kristen said, looking back and forth at her parents.

"Just not good enough to get a phone call," Jule smiled.

Kristen was sure Mr. Banks would call eventually and he just hadn't got around to it.

"As for you my imaginative son, Ms. Annadale is very proud of you."

Jule looked across the table at Kristen who wouldn't look in his direction. She hated being outdone by anyone, especially her brother.

After supper, Jule sat at his desk trying to do homework but all he could think of was the steelhead the osprey seemed to be showing him, as it flew by. Thinking back, there was no denying it. The bird had intentionally flown by him clutching the fish, like he wanted him to see it. Even stranger, was the osprey slightly turning its head to make eye contact with him. Jule could still feel its sharp, bright yellow eyes boring directly into his as it flew by. A distinct shiver went up and down his spine as he thought about the experience. *Maybe I just imagined it.* Still, he wished he could catch a fish like that. One thing's for sure, the osprey proved there are big fish in the river and he couldn't be happier. Jule could hardly wait to get fishing again.

He closed his math book and went over to his bed to lie down. He lay quietly with his fingers locked behind his head, studying the illuminated posters of the universe that covered the bedroom ceiling. Though fishing was his favourite past time, astronomy was a close second. He would love to venture anywhere through space, especially to Pluto. *One day I will.* With his eyes focused on Pluto, he reached down under his bed and pulled out his latest astronomy magazine tearing into the plastic wrapper. "What!" he said bolting upright as he read the headline: 'New World Found Beyond Pluto'.

2

THE NEXT DAY Ms. Annadale asked the students to sit down at their desks. She stood at the front of the class waving a sheet of paper in her hand, waiting for the kids to settle. "I have read all your stories about the places you would like to visit. Some of you would like to visit Africa, California, Italy and France. Others wrote about spending time up in the mountains or visiting Toronto. Some wrote about their favourite mall. Generally, they were all good stories. But, there was one in particular that was excellent. This student took me beyond our world and wrote from his heart about a place I would certainly like to visit." The kids looked at each other trying to figure out whose story Ms. Annadale liked the best. Finally after some guessing, she called upon Jule to share his special place with the class. He wished she would read it, as he hated being centered out. He walked quickly to Ms. Annadale to get his story and began reading.

Peaceful Pluto

"When Pluto was discovered in 1930, it was called a planet because it occupied the void beyond Neptune. Today, scientists are debating whether Pluto should remain a planet because of its size. Personally, I think they should uphold the 74-year tradition of our solar system containing nine planets, because Pluto is the best planet in the universe and I will tell you why I would love to visit it."

He was just about to read the next sentence when a honeybee landed under the first word of it. He wasn't sure what to do so he continued reading slowly, hoping it would fly away. "Peaceful Pluto is a place where man has not interfered." The golden brown striped bee kept pace with each word he read. "Therefore, birds of many shades of orange, lime, fuchsia, mauve, yellow and turquoise fly freely throughout trees that never die." Again, the bee passed under each word. There was no doubt, when he stopped reading, the bee stopped walking. But what really caught his eye, was how the bee's translucent wings reflected a rainbow of colours from the ceiling lights.

"Jule. Is there something wrong?" Ms. Annadale asked. He seemed distracted and was reading each word so slowly. She knew he was a much better reader than that.

He wasn't sure whether to tell her about the bee. He looked toward Ms. Annadale. "There's a bee on my paper." But when he looked down at the paper, the bee was gone. "I guess it flew away," he smiled, continuing to read. "The water is clean. There is no need to carry around bottled water because you can kneel down beside any river or lake and drink handfuls. Lakes and streams are full of big, healthy, mercury-free fish. Animals such as bear and deer wander freely. There are no smog days. The air is always fresh with smells of pine needles and forests after a summer rain. Food that has not been processed with chemicals or preservatives is plentiful. No one diets or spends time worrying about how they look, because they always feel good about themselves. Malls and televisions don't exist, so no one wastes precious time. People are always friendly. They don't care what you look like and never say a bad word about others. Kindness rules. No one works, so they are never too busy to spend time with their family. There is no school. You are your own teacher and you learn from all the adventures that await you. If you want to see the sun and feel its warmth, all you have to do is turn the other cheek. Zillions of stars shine at night and even during the day, like sparkly diamonds that totally surround you. There is no violence or hate. Just peace."

As he returned to his seat, his classmates applauded and his teacher thanked him for sharing his special place with the class.

When the recess bell sounded, the kids filed out into the bright sunshine. Jule put his baseball glove on his left hand and started punching it with his right looking to see if a baseball game had started up. He spotted some kids in the field and it looked like they were just starting to choose the teams. He was just about to leave the pavement area when he stopped and watched some older boys harassing a girl. They continued chanting and circling her trying to pull up her dress. He thought about ignoring them and continuing out to the baseball field, but he couldn't see the teacher that was on yard duty. The five boys were relentless with their tormenting and chants. "Janet is a fat slob. Janet is a fat slob."

"Leave her alone," Jule said, walking up behind the instigator, punching his glove.

"And who's going to stop me?" the tall boy said, spinning around on his heel to find out who would dare question him.

"It won't be necessary for anyone to stop you, if you leave her alone," Jule said, standing as tall as he could. Even then he had to look up at him. Janet stood close by wiping her tears with her sleeve and straightening her dress.

"She's fat and I don't like the look of her," he said, with his face a few centimeters from Jule's.

Yuk! More bad breath. Don't these kids ever brush their teeth? "Maybe she doesn't like the look of you," he said, holding back a gag.

"You're really brave for a little grade, whatever, jerk."

"And you're quite stupid for a big grade, whatever, jerk."

"Why you ..." The boy was just about to swing at Jule when a honey bee landed on his forehead distracting him. Jule saw it as an opportunity to get in the first punch and wasted no time, as he reached up connecting a hard right to the kid's left cheek, scattering the bee. Before the kid had a chance to swing back, the teacher on yard duty had them both by the back of their shirts. The boys turned around in unison and found themselves in the tight grip of the 6'5" Ms. Brocklehurst. With broader shoulders than an Argonaut fullback and a surly disposition to match, the school's French teacher was not amused. They knew they were in deep trouble as she carted them off to the principal's office.

"You both know we don't tolerate fighting at our school," she said, with her hazel eyes bulging slightly. She loosened her grip once they were inside. "Tyler, you sit on this side," she said, pointing to two red vinyl chairs lined up against the wall just outside the main office. "What's your name, son?" she asked quickly, turning toward Jule. He was sure she was frothing at the mouth as he told her his name.

"Fine, Jule. You take that second chair. Move it to the other side of the hall then sit and wait for the principal to come back."

They both sat quietly and listened as Ms. Brocklehurst made her way back down the hallway clicking her heels heavily on the terrazzo floor with each step.

Tyler waited until she was out of sight. "Nice going jerk. I had better not get in trouble with the principal because of you." He glared at Jule with his piercing dark blue eyes. This wasn't the first time that Tyler Watson had seen the inside of the principal's office. He flicked back his black wavy hair before resting his arms on the top of his legs and leaning forward, continuing his rant. "What a stupid name you have. Juuuule. Maybe your parents meant to call you Julie instead 'cause you punch like a sissy girl."

Jule stared at the large bruise that covered most of Tyler's left cheek. He was tempted to tell him about it, but decided that a mirror would do a better job. Instead, he chose to ignore him by focusing on the beige switch plate just above Tyler's head, wishing he was fishing down by the river, instead of sitting across from this jerk. If Ms. Brocklehurst hadn't come along to stop the fight, he would probably have skipped off school and run to the river.

"Well you two, I hear from Ms. Brockelhurst that there was some fighting going on in the school yard," the principal said, looking back and forth between them. "I'm going to have to talk with each of you," he said, straightening his burgundy and silver tie. He buttoned his navy blazer, as he asked Tyler to follow him into his office.

Jule sat thinking about the incident, examining his leather baseball glove. He knew now, he should have ignored it and continued out onto the field instead of interfering with Tyler and his stupid friends. That girl could have gone to Ms. Brocklehurst and she would have straightened everything out. He thought about his opportunity to get the first punch in and remembered the honey bee. If it hadn't landed on

Tyler's forehead, he would have probably been worse off. Then there was the bee landing on his Peaceful Pluto story. Jule concluded it was all a coincidence, as springtime and honey bees are synonymous.

"Well Tyler, from the looks of your face, you seem to have gotten the worst of it," Mr. Coulter said, noting his bruised cheek. "After I speak with you, have my secretary, Mrs. Campbell, get you some ice for it. In the meantime Tyler, tell me *exactly* what happened?" He made a point of exaggerating 'exactly'.

"Well Sir, me and some of my friends were just standing around talking to some of the girls we know when Julie, I, I mean Jule, came up and interrupted our rap session. Seems he didn't like what he was hearing."

"What exactly were you saying to the girls?"

Tyler was unprepared for the question and had to think of a quick answer. "Well sir," he continued killing time as he thought, "we were telling them about our baseball team and that it was the best in the school, thanks to our teacher Mr. Banks. Well, it seems Jule didn't think so. When I asked what his problem was, he punched me in the face," Tyler said, touching his purple cheek. *That little rat really did clobber me.* His face was quite sore. *Might as well milk this one.* "So you see sir, I was just trying to get to the bottom of Jule's problem, when he hauled off and hit me," he said, gingerly rubbing his cheek.

Mr. Coulter sat back in his chair after writing down a few notes. "That's all for now Tyler. You can go see Mrs. Campbell. Would you please ask Jule to come in on your way out?"

"Yes sir."

"Mr. Coulter would like to see you now," Tyler said politely. "You're dead meat," he whispered, as Jule passed by him.

Jule entered the principal's office and sat down on one of the two black chrome chairs, separated by a small wooden table displaying some school trophies. The wall behind the filing cabinet was lined with pictures of Mr. Coulter holding up different sized fish he had caught. He looked up from his notes. "I'd like to hear your side of what happened at recess," he said, turning to face Jule, who was still staring at the pictures. He wanted to say something about them. Instead, he turned toward the principal. "They were bullying one of the girls."

"Who?"

"Tyler and some of his friends."

"Which girl?"

Jule tried to recall the girl's name and soon realized that he couldn't. *Great.* "I don't know her name," he sighed, sitting back heavily in the chair.

The principal looked Jule in the eye. "Being expelled for someone that you don't even know is a quite high price to pay for hitting Tyler, don't you think?"

"No." Jule thought for a second. "I mean yes."

"Which is it?"

"Yes."

"According to Tyler, you walked up and interrupted the conversation he and his friends were having with some girls. It seems you didn't like what they were talking about. Is that true?"

Jule leaned forward in his chair and stared at his baseball glove still on his left hand. *After Tyler's lies, it won't matter what I say. The principal probably won't believe me anyway.* "It's true."

Though Mr. Coulter figured there was probably more to the story, he only had Tyler's account of it.

"You know the rule son. No fighting allowed at our school. I am going to have to call your parents and speak with them about this incident and your suspension. For now, you are to go back to class," he said, getting up from his desk. As Jule passed by the principal, he was tempted to continuing walking right out of the school.

Just then, the girl he had defended at recess came running into the main office stopping in front of him. " I don't know who you are, but I want to thank you for stopping Tyler and his friends from bullying me. No one has ever stood up for me before."

"Is that what you were doing, Jule?" the principal asked, overhearing their conversation.

"Yes, Mr. Coulter," she continued, before he had a chance to answer. "Tyler was making fun of me, like he always does. Him and his friends. They never leave me alone," she said, breaking down and starting to cry.

Mr. Coulter came out to the main office and asked Jule to sit beside the secretary's desk then asked the girl to have a seat in his office. Through her tears, she told him about the incident in the school yard at recess. The principal thanked her for coming to the office and telling him what really happened. He figured that there must have been more to this. When Tyler Watson is involved, there always is. Mr. Coulter promised to discipline those involved then sent her back to class.

"Jule, will you please come in," the principal called out from his desk. "The girl you gallantly rescued this morning is Janet Evans. She told me how you went to her defense when Tyler and his friends were harassing her. I admire the fact that you tried to stop the incident, but it was the method you used that concerns me. You know that there is absolutely no fighting on school property."

"Yes sir."

"I am not suspending you. But, I will be calling your parents, as this incident will go on your school records. And, if this happens again, no matter what the circumstances, you will be suspended. Do you understand?"

"Yes sir." He was thankful he wasn't going to be suspended, but still there was the phone call to his parents and the disciplining that would follow, probably no fishing for who knows how long.

He sent Jule back to class and asked Mrs. Campbell to have Tyler Watson report to the office immediately.

At the end of the school day, the bus pulled up in front of the house. Jule stood on the bus doorstep watching as Kristen walked quickly to the back door. She couldn't wait to open her big mouth and tell Mom about the incident with Tyler. "Well, Jule's done it this time," she said, hanging her jacket on the coat hook by the door.

"I have already spoken with the principal, Kristen," Mom said, cutting her off.

"I am so embarrassed. Tyler Watson is a really nice guy," she continued, gulping for air. She was already on a roll when Jule walked in the door.

"He's a jerk," Jule said, hanging his backpack on another hook.

Kristen turned to face her brother. "You're the jerk!"

"That's enough Kristen!" Mom cut in.

"Well he is. It's always my brother getting into trouble. You're going to have to do something before he completely ruins me."

Lately, Kristen had been crowned drama queen, as even the slightest upset became a major issue. "Aren't you overreacting, just a little, dear?"

"No, I'm not!" she yelled, stomping out of the kitchen. They both watched as Kristen swung the door to the hallway so wide, it hit the wall before bouncing back and closing.

Mom turned to Jule. "No sense asking how your day went." She had been caught off guard when she got the call from Mr. Coulter. It was so out of character for Jule to be in a fight that she had a good cry after she hung up the phone. "This fighting business is very serious," she said. It was difficult to think he was a fighter. He has always been so kind and gentle.

Jule thought back to the incident with Tyler. He was proud he'd thrown a most deserving punch, as the creep needed to be stopped. "I know Mom. I won't fight in the school yard anymore."

"Can I hold you to that?"

"Yes." *Unless Tyler gets in my face.*

"I am proud of you for standing up for Janet, though you shouldn't have fought about it."

"It shouldn't have happened in the first place, Mom. No one has the right to say anything bad about anyone. Can I go fishing?" he said, quickly changing the subject. He hated confrontations with anyone. After all that happened at school, he really needed the tranquility of his thinking place in the woods.

Mom couldn't believe he was asking to go fishing. Obviously, he doesn't see the seriousness of this. "No Jule. You are staying put today. Do you have any homework?"

"A bit."

"Then I suggest you go to your room and do it."

Jule's Story

What a day. He scooped his backpack off the hook and walked upstairs to his bedroom and sat down hard on his bed. *Girls.* If it wasn't his mother waking him every morning, or his sister freaking out every second, there was the snake girl and now the fat girl who he almost got expelled for. *Why doesn't everyone just leave me alone?* The predicted knock on his door interrupted his rant. "Come in."

"Hello Jule." He could tell by his dad's tone, he was going to get a lecture. "I hear you've had quite a day at school. You do understand the seriousness of this," he said, sitting down beside him on the edge of the bed.

First Mom. Now Dad. "Yes."

"And you realize that the next time you will be expelled."

"There won't be a next time, Dad. I already promised Mom."

His dad wasn't convinced he was sincere about his promise. "As punishment, for the remainder of this week, when you get home from school, you are to stay in your room until dinner."

He knew he would be punished for punching Tyler, but had hoped for a lighter sentence. That meant four days of good fishing would be wasted.

Dad could tell by the look on his face that he wasn't happy. "This is a very serious matter, Jule. Your mom and I believe that some sort of punishment is in order. This isn't the first time we've heard from the school."

"I don't skip school anymore," Jule said, staring at the floor.

"And now you can add no fighting. I just have one other question, son. Why didn't you tell the principal exactly what happened when he asked you?"

Jule looked up toward the galaxy posters on his ceiling thinking about his talk with Mr. Coulter. He had wanted to tell him his side of the story, but judging by the principal's accusing tone he would probably believe Tyler, especially with the massive bruise on his cheek. There was no sense trying to change Mr. Coulter's mind. "I didn't think he'd believe me." But he was thankful Janet had appeared in the office to set the record straight. Otherwise, the principal may never have known what really happened.

"Well thankfully Mr. Coulter was able to get it all sorted out," Dad said walking toward the door. He stopped and turned to face Jule. "Remember son, the truth always comes out in the end."

3

JULE RAN AS fast as his legs would go to his thinking place in the woods. Breathless, he sat down hard on an old, moss-covered log. *I am never going back to that stupid school. I hate Tyler. I hate them all. I am staying here in the woods. This is where I belong.* He covered his face with his hands as big sobs got the better of him.

"Why are you crying?"

Jule looked up from his cupped hands wondering where his own voice was coming from. Not only did this individual sound like him, but he totally looked like him. A complete identical replica of himself was sitting on a log not more than four metres away. He rubbed his eyes and thought they must be out of focus with all the tears. *This can't be.* He began quickly blinking his eyes. "I must be seeing things," he said, wiping away his tears with dirty hands.

"No, you are not seeing things."

He talks just like me. "Is this some kind of a joke? You look and sound just like me."

"Well, I am your duplicate, only my face is cleaner," he smiled.

He has the same dimpled smile. Jule's eyes widened as he sat studying him from head to toe. *He has my brown eyes and my straight dark brown hair, cut exactly the same way.* His mind raced as he tried to think of something that would make them nonidentical. *This will.* "What happens to your hair when you sweat?"

He anticipated Jule's question. "It goes curly."

Jule reeled backward on the log. It was exactly what happened to his hair when he perspired. He thought he must be dreaming so he pinched his arm to verify he wasn't. He took a deep breath sitting up straight on the log, as his replica followed his lead and did the same. *This is crazy* he thought, continuing with his questions. "Where did you come from?" he asked, wiping his face with a hankie.

"I come from a place just beyond your imagination."

What a stupid answer. "Do you have a name?" Jule asked impatiently, leaning forward to take a closer look.

"Jule."

Jule looked up at the tallest white pine tree then back at his twin. *This can't be.* "That's my name. I was named after my grandfather, Jule."

"Me too."

Jule sat dumbfounded wondering if the kids make fun of his name too. "Do you hate your name? The kids at school make fun of mine and call me Julie. I guess the kids make fun of you too."

"In answer to your first question, I don't hate my name. On the contrary, I am very proud of it and secondly, the kids don't make fun of my name, because we respect each other."

"Now, that's where we differ. The kids were making fun of me just this morning at recess and that's why I ended up here." Jule's head was spinning, as he continued with his interrogation. "Why aren't you in school?"

"I ask you the same question?" his double said.

Jule's Story

"I skipped out at recess. I needed to come to my thinking place. Do you have a thinking place?"

"Yes, I do."

"Well, this is my thinking place. I love being here in the woods with nature. Lately, it's the only place I am happy and I can be myself. My grade two teacher once said I would be better off on my own, away from everybody. My sister thinks I'm weird."

"That means, if you are weird, I am weird."

This whole thing is weird. I came here to be alone and end up being with myself. Jule ran his hands through his hair. "I am nine years old, almost ten. How old are you?"

"The same plus one million."

"Today I feel that old too," he said, watching as a vole quickly ran from one dead log to another. He had to think of something else that they wouldn't have in common then remembered the birthmark on his arm. *There's no way he will have this*, he thought rolling up his left sleeve. "I have this large, dark brown birth mark just above my left elbow. The doctor said I have to keep an eye on it to make sure it doesn't get any bigger. It could develop into skin cancer when I'm older." Jule watched as his twin began rolling up the sleeve of his beige shirt, revealing the identical birthmark just above his right elbow.

"Wow! I thought I was the only person on earth to have one," he said, rolling his sleeve back down and buttoning the cuff. *This guy really is a duplicate of me.*

They sat quietly on their respective logs staring at each other. *Here's the real test* Jule thought confidently. "If you are me, what are some of the things you like to do?" he asked, breaking the silence.

His twin didn't hesitate to answer. "Today, I'm connecting with nature, and I may go fishing."

"No way! You are like me! Connecting with nature and fishing are my favourite pastimes." *At least I've got a smart twin*, he decided.

"Mine too. Would you like to do some fishing?"

"I wish, but I don't have my fishing rod here and if I go home I'll get into trouble for skipping school, again. That's going to happen sooner or later anyway 'cause Ms. Annadale would have called my mom by now." He watched as his duplicate reached behind the log he sat on. "Will this do?"

Jule's eyes widened as he jumped up from the log and ran toward him. "Wow! That's a Shakespeare Ugly Stik. They are the best! I keep asking for one for my birthday, but my dad says the rod is too good for someone my age. It must have cost a bomb!"

"Cost a bomb?" his twin said, handing him the rod. He had never heard such a saying before.

"It means very expensive," Jule said, running his hand over its length. He had never seen anything as beautiful in his whole life. The black rubber handgrip was a perfect fit for his hand.

"Happy birthday, Jule."

"What!" He couldn't believe what he was hearing.

"The Ugly Stik is all yours," his twin smiled.

"Are you sure?" *This must be some sort of joke.* But his twin just stood there nodding. "Wow! Thank you so much! Just for that, I am going to take you to my secret fishing place."

They walked quickly along the path marked with the old shoelace through some dense woods until they came to a clearing by the river. They stood quietly and watched as a large cow moose and her calf stuck their heads underwater to scoop mouthfuls of slimy weeds from the riverbed on the opposite side. Their presence didn't go unnoticed, as the mother cautiously began leading her calf back toward higher brush.

"We can sit on these two large rocks, or we can sit over there on that fallen poplar tree," Jule whispered, trying not to disturb the moose and her young one.

His twin stood at the river's edge and looked back and forth then concluded that this was a good spot, but if they moved down river about 30 meters there would be much better fishing. Jule followed closely behind as they made their way along the shore. They finally came to a stop just around the bend where there was a much deeper, fast flowing current. Jule glanced around the area and decided that this must be the place where the osprey scooped the fish, before flying by him that day. He turned to his duplicate. "We don't have any bait." He watched as his twin opened his shirt pocket, reaching in and pulling out a clear small fly box. "I don't suppose you would happen to have a No. 10 Hare's Ear Nymph?"

"Here you are," he said, handing it over.

"Oh my goodness!" *This is definitely a dream* he thought, attaching it to the line.

Jule cast off, lobbing the fly to the inside edge of the main flow, starting a drift. No sooner had the rig hit the water when a steelhead began thrashing around on the end of his line. "I've got one!" he yelled, running further downstream to the next pool to beach it. He was sure it was a four-pounder by the way it fought back. His new Shakespeare Ugly Stik made landing it a breeze. Once the fish was on shore, he turned to his duplicate and smiled. "I've never been this lucky! Probably because I have always used roe for bait."

"My experience has been that flies out fish any bait," he smiled, admiring Jule's catch.

"I don't have my stringer," Jule said, standing very still holding the trout through both gills calming the fish.

"You don't need one," his twin replied, pulling out his shiny red pocket knife.

Jule's eyes widened when he saw the knife. "I have the exact same knife. I left it at home. Knives aren't allowed at school. That would mean instant expulsion."

"Responsibility has its privileges," his twin said, wandering around looking for a downed tree branch.

Jule watched as he picked up a thick curved birch branch and expertly whittled the end to a point. When he finished, he held up a sturdy 80 centimeter long wooden hook that was identical to a fish hook or a capital 'J'. "May I?" he said, taking the fish and mounting it through its left gill and out the mouth.

"Wow! That was awesome. You can't be me. I would never have thought of that."

"Now you will," he replied, placing the mounted fish so it hung between two large boulders.

"I can't believe I caught the fish," Jule said, as they stood by the river's edge. "The only time I have ever seen a fish that size in the river, was when an osprey scooped one in its talons. It flew right by me with it a couple of weeks ago. I was sitting right down there," he said, pointing downstream, remembering the experience like it was only yesterday.

"You enjoyed that, eh?" his twin said, noting the sparkle in his eye.

"It was awesome! I remember thinking I wish I could do that. And now I have. If I didn't know any better, I would say it was the same fish. But it can't be," Jule said, turning toward his twin. Though this was definitely the best time of his life so far, he had to go home. He knew he was in a heap of trouble for skipping school. Especially when he promised his parents that he wouldn't anymore. But, if he brought home his twin, his parents probably wouldn't be as angry. "How would you like to have dinner at my house?"

"I would like that."

Jule breathed a sigh of relief. His parents would never cause a scene in front of company. "Great. Do you have a second name?"

"Albert."

Once again, Jule was stunned by his answer, but he shouldn't have been. After all, he is his exact twin. "It's my second name also. I was named after my other grandfather. My mom's dad."

"Me too."

This is all so strange. Jule wasn't sure what was going on and didn't have time to find out. "We had better get going. Come with me Albert and I will take you home to meet my family. But watch out for my sister," he said, turning to collect the fish. Jule's eyes just about popped out of his head when he turned around. "Albert! Don't make any sudden moves," Jule whispered in a trembling voice. They stood very still and watched as a large black bear sniffed his way toward them. Jule knew he should make himself as large as possible and start making lots of noise to try and scare the bear off. Instead, he backed away slowly and watched as Albert stood fearlessly by the fish. He tried to call Albert back, but he was so frightened nothing would come out of his mouth. With less than a metre between Albert and the advancing bear, he raised his left hand and it stopped suddenly, as if hypnotized. Shakily, it attempted to stand up on its hind legs to voice itself, but remained silent. After a few seconds of trying to growl, Albert slowly lowered his hand. The bear suddenly fell back on its butt with a heavy thud. Stunned, it looked up at Albert, turned, and then quickly ran back into the woods.

Jule couldn't believe what he had just witnessed. And when he questioned Albert, he acted like nothing had happened. "That bear was going to attack you to get the fish!"

"No, he wouldn't. He just wanted to congratulate you on your catch," Albert said, handing him the mounted trout. "Shall I carry your fishing rod? You may need two hands to carry the fish."

"Yes, please," Jule said, shaking his head in disbelief, as he handed him the rod.

They chatted back and forth making their way back along the path through the woods. Jule was surprised by how much alike they really are. They had so much in common that there was no doubt they were twins. "Do you come here often?" Albert asked.

"As often as I can. No one knows about my secret place, except you. Now I have another secret place, thanks to you. I have tried many times to bring my dad here, but he is always too busy."

"Maybe one day he won't be," Albert said confidently, as they proceeded down the road. "You keep going. I have to tie my shoe."

Jule turned and watched as Albert bent over to tie his shoe before continuing on slowly hanging on tightly to the 'J' shaped stick. He was just about to ask him how he knew about that fishing spot down river when his father quickly rounded the corner. He could tell even from this distance that his father was not pleased.

"There you are! Do you have any idea what time it is?" he asked breathlessly.

"I forgot my watch, but I can explain," Jule said, staring up at his father's angry face. "Do you think you are seeing double?"

"All I see is a young lad who is in a heap of trouble."

"Dad, look behind me," he said, motioning with his head.

He looked over his son's head, his eyes following the pavement. "Well, isn't that strange."

"See Dad! That's my twin," Jule smiled, watching for his father's reaction.

"Really," he said, watching a ruffed grouse with its elongated neck run quickly across the road. "Seems that grouse knows when it's dinnertime and doesn't upset its parents with worry."

"What!" Jule cried, turning as the grouse began pecking through the sand for bits of gravel. *That can't be. Albert was just there tying his shoe.*

"Come on son! We are really late for supper and your mother is very upset," he said, pulling him along. "But Dad, aren't you wondering where I got this fish from?"

"No! You can explain everything at supper. Now move it!"

It was all Jule could do to hang on to the mounted fish and keep up with his father, who periodically nudged him to move faster.

When they got to the back door, Mom was waiting as they walked up the steps. The angry look on her face said it all, as she handed the mounted fish to Dad and told Jule to quickly wash up for dinner.

"How gross. Your face is sooooo dirty," Kristen said, walking on tip toes to get by him in the hall.

"Whatever," he said, making a silly face before shutting the bathroom door. He quickly washed up, then quietly took his place at the dinner table across from Kristen. He could tell by the look on his parent's faces that this time he was in major trouble. He was confident that telling them about Albert would dissolve their anger. "I am not sure where to begin, Jule," Mom sighed, passing him the wooden salad bowl.

"You're in big trouble." As usual, Kristen had to put her two-cents worth in and thankfully Dad wasted no time telling her to be quiet and eat. The last thing Jule needed was her yapping.

"Your teacher called, again. I hope you have a good explanation," Mom continued. "Not to mention all the worry you have put us through."

Now's my chance he thought smirking across the table at Kristen who was staring right back. "I was fishing with my twin."

"Huh! Now, there's a good story! You are so weird."

"Kristen, that's enough!" Dad barked.

"It's not a story, Kristen," Jule continued, cutting his roast beef. "My twin gave me a Shakespeare Ugly Stik for my birthday."

"Oh sure! Where's this rod? Sounds like a story to me," Kristen said, rolling her blue eyes, as she looked toward the ceiling.

"How do you think I caught the fish?" he smiled, looking in Kristen's direction.

"You don't believe all this stupid twin stuff, do you?" Kristen said, looking back and forth at Mom and Dad.

Mom didn't know what to believe she was so upset. Dad just stared down at his plate.

"Mom says everyone has a twin," he continued.

"Jule Desjoux, you are the biggest jerk I have ever known. That is just a saying." Kristen said, staring at him from across the table.

"Where you're concerned, I hope it is just a saying. I couldn't stand two of you," Jule replied, staring back.

"Okay. Jule, that's enough!" Dad snapped angrily.

"I'm sick of her. Kristen puts her nose into everything and never keeps her mouth shut!"

"That's it! Excuse yourself and go to your room."

Jule excused himself as he pushed his chair back and left it. He stomped out of the kitchen, up the stairs, and slammed his bedroom door. He kicked off his shoes then sat down heavily on the bed. He couldn't understand why they didn't believe him. He was telling the truth. He stretched out on his bed to study his galaxy posters on the ceiling and spotted Pluto, wondering if Albert was interested in outer space. The inevitable knock on the door interrupted his thoughts. "Enter," he said, remaining horizontal.

His dad closed the door then sat down on the edge of the bed holding the stick the fish had been mounted on. "I thought we were through with all this nonsense last week and you weren't going to skip school anymore," he said, placing the 'J' shaped stick on the floor.

Jule lay still, his gaze locked on the ceiling, wishing he was flying through the universe, preferably on his way to Pluto. *How can I tell him I hate my name because the kids at school call me Julie? It's so embarrassing and now I to have to explain it.* "I was having a bad day at school, and I needed to go to my thinking place."

"Your sister said some of the older kids were making fun of your name at recess. Is this true?"

It figures that Kristen would have to stick her big nose where it doesn't belong. "Yes."

"Do you think running away is the answer?"

"No, but it's better than fighting," he said, turning to face his dad.

"That's true. But, better still, staying at school and ignoring them."

His dad had no idea how hard he tried to ignore them. But it was pretty difficult when you had four or five kids chanting Julie in your face. "They call me Julie all the time. Do you know how embarrassing that is? It makes me wish my name was Brian or Doug?" Anything but Jule.

Dad leaned back on his hands and gazed up at the ceiling posters and proceeded to explain why they had called him Jule. "As you know, we named you after your grandfather, who was a great man, admired by all who knew him. We gave you a special name, because you are a very special son. And one thing's for sure, Grandpa would be very proud of his namesake."

"Did the kids make fun of Grandpa?"

"I doubt it." *He would probably have hauled off and bopped them one.* "Son, if the name calling happens again, try to ignore them. But don't leave school. Go to the teacher on yard duty or the principal's office to report the incident."

Sure Dad. He had no idea what it was like. The kids were never going to stop. "I won't leave school anymore. You have my word."

"I'm counting on that." Dad stood up to leave stepping on the stick. He was surprised it didn't snap in two. "By the way, I fileted your fish. It was some catch. Close to four pounds," he said, picking up the stick examining the point. "You did quite a whittling job, Son."

"I didn't do it, Dad. My twin did." Jule could tell by the look on Dad's face that he didn't believe him.

"Right," he sighed, hanging it on the bedpost. He was too tired to argue. "It's time to get ready for bed. You have school tomorrow, and you are going. And staying," he said, firmly looking Jule in the eye. "Night, Son."

Jule's Story

"Night Dad." Jule got washed and ready for bed, thinking about his time with Albert. He grabbed the stick the trout had been mounted on and lay in bed examining it. One thing's for sure, Albert is fast and accurate with a pocket knife. He thought about the episode with the bear. Albert was in full control of it. It was like it was hypnotized or something. That bear wanted the fish so badly, it was frothing at the mouth. But suddenly it fell on its butt, got up then ran for its life. It was amazing. Jule decided then and there, he never wanted to get that close to a bear again. He had never been so frightened in his life. And what about this twin Albert? It was so strange meeting up with one's twin. *He's exactly like me. He wore the same beige shirt and dark-brown khaki pants. His haircut was identical to mine. And when he perspired his hair curled too. My connection with nature and fishing is mirrored by Albert. He even has a thinking place.* Jule wondered where Albert's thinking place was. But most of all, where did he come from? 'I come from a place just beyond your imagination'. He wondered what Albert meant by that. And when his dad came around the bend, where did he go? It seemed like he disappeared into thin air. He remembered the fishing rod Albert gave him for his birthday and wondered what happened to it. There were so many unanswered questions.

Jule got out of bed, pulling back the curtains to look at the starlit sky. It was a calm, warm, late spring evening with only the monotonous flute-like whistle of a northern saw-whet owl calling its mate breaking the silence. He enjoyed its musical love call that often lolled him to sleep, as it would continue throughout the night. He took deep breaths, as he scanned the diamond-speckled sky. There was a bright beam of light seeming to originate from the heavens, targeting and illuminating one particular oak tree that caught his eye. He had never seen anything like it before, as he pressed his forehead against the screen to get a better look. He traced the brilliant light down to the bottom branch where the intense light was directed. *What?* He pressed his head heavily against the screen almost dislodging it. His heart started racing. Resting on the bottom branch of the oak tree was the Shakespeare Ugly Stik Albert had given him.

4

JULE RAN QUICKLY back to bed, pulling the covers up when he heard the knock on his door, wondering who it could be. "Yes," he said, trying to catch his breath from all the excitement.

"I just came up to say good night," Mom said, sitting down on the edge of the bed. Jule lay with the covers up over his mouth and nose trying not to breathe too hard. "Are you okay?" she asked, placing her hand on his forehead.

"Yeah, fine."

"You seem a little warm."

"I'm fine, Mom," he said, as his breathing calmed.

"Dad told me about the discussion you two had. We had no idea that you didn't like your name."

"I do like my name." He didn't want to talk to her about it. All he wanted to do was get back to the window and see his Shakespeare Ugly Stik. "I'm really tired Mom."

"Okay Son. I'll see you in the morning. Love you."

This would have been the perfect time to discuss her morning wake-up routine, but all he wanted to do was get back to the window.

"Shall I close the curtains? It seems awfully bright outside. There must be a full moon," she said, walking toward the window.

"No, it's fine Mom! I like the brightness," he said, trying to stop her.

She reached for the curtains then stopped. "That's odd," she said, looking intently out the window.

"What Mom?" Jule asked, sitting upright.

"I thought I saw ... no it's just my imagination."

Jule was afraid to ask. "What Mom?"

"Oh my goodness, it is! You gotta see this! Hurry, come here!" She didn't have to ask him twice as he sprang from his bed and ran to the window, his heart pounding in his chest as he stood beside her.

"See!" she cried.

"See what, Mom?" he swallowed.

"The neighbor's cat! It's chasing that nuisance raccoon around the old birch tree. I can't believe it! Look, there they go!"

They watched as the raccoon scaled the side of the shed, with the cat close behind it, then across the roof and down the other side out of sight. Jule looked up at the full moon that illuminated the sky, replacing the bright beam that had shone on the oak tree. *There are some strange things happening around here* he concluded as he got back into bed.

After his mom left the room, Jule ran to the window and opened the curtains. It was really dark now and he couldn't see the tree. The moon was covered with clouds, but a sudden flash of lightning turned the night into day. He stood at the window waiting for the next flash and spotted the tree his fishing rod was in. He waited for more flashes of lightning and spotted it sitting on the bottom branch. *I have to retrieve the Ugly Stik before anyone else finds it.* He glanced at the

Jule's Story

clock radio on his night table. It was only ten o'clock. His parents usually stay up until eleven, so that eliminated going out the back door. The only choice left was to climb out his bedroom window onto the roof of the family room, cross over it to the wooden morning glory trellis at the far corner of the house and climb down it. *Piece of cake*, he thought, running over to his bed to get the long black tubular flashlight from underneath it. As a precaution, he took his spare pillow and tucked the covers around it so it looked as if he was in bed. Then he placed his dark brown furry bear under the covers so it looked like the top of his head resting on the pillow. *If I didn't know any better, I would think that was me.*

    He quietly tiptoed over to the window, slid the screen sideways then climbed out onto the great room roof, as lightning flashed and distant thunder began rumbling. He knew he had to hurry, as the speed of a thunderstorm is always unpredictable. He sat down on his butt and inched his way over to the trellis nailed to the back wall. He shone his flashlight on it to make sure it was where he remembered. Mom's morning glory seeds were just starting to grow so he'd have to be careful not to damage the new growth. He could easily jump from one of the lower rungs once he climbed down it. At the edge of the roof, Jule turned onto his stomach, and dangled his legs over the edge until one foot came to rest on the trellis. Moving ever so slightly, he placed his other foot beside it and proceeded to climb down, as lightning flashed illuminating the area. Jumping to the ground narrowly missing the garden, he realized his flashlight was on the roof. It didn't matter, as the intensity of the lightning increased, turning night into day. He ran quickly toward the oak tree with each flash guiding him. Once under the tree, he soon discovered he wasn't tall enough to reach the branch. He searched frantically for the green wrought iron bench that usually sat under it. With the next flash, he saw it a few metres away and proceeded to drag it under the branch where the fishing rod was. Standing as tall as he could, he was still an arm's length away and realized the only way to reach it was to climb onto the branch. Lightning was flashing steadily as he struggled to pull the bench closer, resting the back of it against the thick girth of the tree. He quickly climbed up on the seat then up onto the back of the bench reaching for the tree branch. Suddenly, there was a blinding flash of lightning followed by an explosion of thunder. "Ahhh!" he screamed losing his balance and falling forward landing on all fours behind the bench. Fortunately, he wasn't hurt, but he soon discovered staying on the ground was no longer an option, as the sky opened up instantly drenching him. Frightened and wet, he aborted his plan and ran as fast as he could toward the house through the pouring rain.

Oblivious to what was happening outside, his parents sat in the great room watching TV when they heard a loud thud. "Did you hear that?" Dad asked, looking across the room at Mom.

"I heard something," she replied.

"It sounded like something hitting the roof out back. Maybe a tree branch or something. That's quite a storm," he said, getting up and looking out the back window. "What the heck!"

"What?" she asked, turning off the television and walking toward him.

"I could have sworn I saw Jule running out back during that last flash of lightning."

"That's impossible," Mom said, joining him at the window. "He's upstairs asleep."

Jule's Story

"Well it sure looked like him," Dad said, heading toward the stairs to investigate. Gently, he opened the bedroom door and glanced at the bed, as a gust of wind blew the curtains well into the room. He quietly walked over and shut the window then tiptoed out again. "You're right dear," he whispered, closing the door, as Mom approached. "He's sound asleep."

Breathless, Jule stood close by the house as the rain continued to pour down. He was totally drenched as he began inching his way toward the trellis then proceeded to quickly climb back up. Up on the roof, he frantically searched for his flashlight as the rain beat down on the shingles. He couldn't locate it and almost slipped off the roof trying. Cautiously, he inched backward on his butt until he reached the bedroom window and found it closed. *Great!* Someone must have come up to his room and closed it. He assumed his decoy must have worked, but consequently, he could very well be spending the night out here on the roof. He tried to open the window and it wouldn't budge. What if it was locked? Frightened and soaking wet, he sat close to the window waiting for the storm to move on. After what seemed like forever the moon appeared from behind the clouds. With all his strength he pulled the window, and thankfully it slid open. Breathing a sigh of relief, he quickly crawled in and pulled the screen back in place, shut the window, and closed the curtains. He removed his wet navy polo pajamas and put on a dry olive green pair. Exhausted, he climbed into bed and fell asleep.

The next morning his mom made her routine entrance. "Morning sleepyhead," she said, heading toward the window to open the curtains. "What's this?" she asked, stumbling over the pile of clothing underneath it.

Jule rolled over just in time to see her pick up his wet pyjamas. In his haste to get to bed last night, he had forgotten to put them in the clothes hamper. He also wished he had taken the time last night to talk to her about this childish morning routine; now seemed as good a time as any. "Mom," he began.

"Your pajamas are all wet," she said, interrupting him. "Jule, how did your pyjamas get wet?"

He could hear his dad's approaching footsteps in the hallway. *Busted.* He was just about to answer when his father stuck his head around the door and hearing his mom's question, he said, "I know how they got wet, dear." He looked over at Jule who was now sitting up in bed wondering what was next. "You aren't going to believe this Son, but I swore I saw you running out back last night during the storm. Because it seemed so real, I came up to make sure you were all right. When I got here, you were sound asleep with your window wide open. The rain was pouring in, so I closed it, but not soon enough. So, that's how his pyjamas got wet," he smiled, looking toward Mom who placed them in the clothes hamper. Once again, she reminded Jule to use it for his dirty clothes.

That was close, he sighed after his parents left the room. He quickly jumped out of bed, ran to the window and looked toward the oak tree. There was steam all over the glass from last night's pounding rain so it was too difficult to see if the Ugly Stik was still there. It was getting late, so retrieving it was out of the question, as he quickly dressed for school.

His school day passed by without incident. Jule was glad it was over, as he waited impatiently to board the bus back home. The day had been a total blur, as all he could focus on was locating the Shakespeare Ugly Stik Albert had given him. When the bus pulled up in front of his house, he was

Jule's Story

first to disembark and ran straight to the back of the house. "Dad!" he cried, surprised to see him up the ladder near the trellis. "What are you doing?"

"Cleaning out the eaves trough. It's full of leaves and twigs. During last night's rain it overflowed. That's not all I found," he said, climbing down the ladder and reaching toward his back pocket.

"My flashlight! Thanks Dad," he said, taking it and running for the backdoor. "Hi Mom," he called out, pulling off his jacket and shoes before running through the kitchen.

"Hi Jule. How was ... school?" she asked, watching him disappear into the hallway.

"Good Mom," he called out, climbing the stairs two at a time. He pushed the bedroom door closed chanting as he ran toward the window. "Please let it be there. Please let it be there," he repeated, reaching for his binoculars from the desk corner. He pulled them out of the case letting it drop to the floor. He was just about to look into them when a knock on the door stopped him. "Yes," he called out impatiently, picking up the case and shoving them back in.

"Is everything okay?" Mom asked from the other side of it.

"Yeah Mom. Everything's fine. I just thought I would get going on my homework," he said, sitting down quickly at his desk as the door opened.

"Well, aren't we studious," she whispered, as she watched him read his science book. "I won't keep you," she said closing it once again. Thankfully, she didn't notice the book was upside down. When she returned to the kitchen, Dad had just come in the back door.

"Did you get the eave's trough cleaned out, dear?"

"Yup. Does Jule seem to be acting a little strange to you?"

"No. Why?"

Arlene Johnston

"Remember that strange noise I heard last night during the storm. Like metal hitting metal?"

Mom nodded.

"Well, I found Jule's flashlight in the eaves trough about a metre from the morning glory trellis."

"Did you ask him how it got there?"

"I didn't get a chance. He just thanked me and ran off."

"He's upstairs doing homework. You can ask him later, Dear. At least you found it for him," she said, pecking his cheek.

Jule stood at his bedroom window holding his breath, focusing his binoculars on the bottom branch of the oak tree. The Shakespeare Ugly Stik was gone.

5

SATURDAY MORNING JULE woke up and glanced at his clock radio. It was just after nine. He lay in bed trying to figure out what happened to the Ugly Stik Albert had given him. *Maybe it was all a figment of my imagination and I just willed it to be in the tree.* He thought back to the storm and was sure it was there just before that wicked flash of lightning struck sending him spiraling to the ground. *So, what happened to it? Maybe someone found it. After all, Dad was out back the day after cleaning the eaves ...*

"Hey birthday boy! Are you getting up?" his dad said, knocking on the door then opening it. "This is a very special day."

Jule sat upright. *Today's my birthday! How many people forget their own date of birth!* He was so obsessed with finding the Ugly Stik, he had completely forgotten it. "I'm getting up right now," he said, scrambling out of bed and grabbing some clean clothes out of the drawer. "I'll be right down," he said quickly dressing as he walked to the bathroom.

"Happy birthday!" his family sang in unison, as Jule walked into the kitchen. They were all sitting at the kitchen table in the bright sunshine waiting. "I guess I slept in," he said, sitting down at the table looking at all the good things to eat.

"Happy Birthday little brother. I made the breakfast this morning," Kristen said, emphasizing 'I'.

"In that case, I probably won't see my eleventh birthday," he chuckled. "Just kidding. Not!" he smiled. "Thanks Sis."

In the middle of the round oak table sat a tray with a platter of crisp bacon, a bowl of scrambled eggs, sliced whole-grain buttered toast, fried potatoes, and cut up pieces of orange and grapefruit dotted with cherries and grapes. The food was passed around and everyone filled their plates, talking and laughing as they ate.

"That was delicious," Dad said, leaning back in his chair, rubbing his stomach. "But I'm stuffed."

"Me too," Jule said, placing the knife and fork on his plate. "Thanks Kristen. It was my best birthday breakfast ever."

"Just for that I'm going to give my present to you now," she said, excusing herself from the table.

Dad leaned over to pick-up the gift lying on the floor to the right of his chair. "Happy birthday, Son. You had better open this one first," he said, handing him a gift wrapped in bright yellow, green and blue paper with matching fluorescent green ribbon encircling it. He sat with the gift in his lap waiting for Kristen to return then began opening it as she sat down. Removing the outside wrap revealed blue tissue paper, bound tightly with some contrasting yellow ribbon. "Who wrapped this?" he asked, continuing to unravel his present.

"Mom and I," Kristen said proudly. "We wanted to keep you in suspense."

He peeled the last of the wrap off then removed the plain cardboard lid, looked into the box, and gasped.

Jule's Story

"Well, what do you think Son?"

Jule stared down at his gift. The mystery had been solved. Dad found the Shakespeare Ugly Stik that Albert had left on the tree branch for him. Though he finally discovered what had happened to it, he was at a loss for words thinking that his parents would re-gift it for his birthday. "It's great. Thanks."

They were all puzzled by his lack of enthusiasm, as he placed the box on the floor beside his chair.

"It is what you wanted, isn't it?" Dad probed.

"Yes."

"Here open my gift," Kristen smiled sweetly. Again, she made sure that opening it would be a difficult task, by using half of a roll of tape. She chuckled as she watched him struggle with the last of the wrap.

He looked down at the small plastic container and stared in disbelief. There was the No. 10 Hare's Ear Nymph Albert had given him. "Thanks Kristen," he said, placing it on top of his other present.

"It goes with the gift from Mom and Dad."

"I can see that, Kristen. May I be excused?"

They sat and watched as he gathered up his gifts and left the kitchen and waited until they heard his bedroom door close. "That was strange," Mom said. "He didn't seem excited about his gifts at all. And they were exactly what he wanted. He's been dropping hints ever since Christmas. Maybe you should go talk to him," she said, looking in Dad's direction.

"I will in a bit. Maybe he's just tired. After all, I did have to wake him up," Dad smiled awkwardly, gathering up the breakfast dishes.

Jule sat on his bed and examined the rod from top to bottom. There was no doubt, it was definitely the rod Albert had left in the oak tree. He examined the No. 10 Hare's Ear

Nymph Kristen had given him. Again, it was the one Albert had pulled out of his pocket a few days ago. Jule attached it to the fishing line. He opened the bedroom window and stood staring at the lower branch of the oak tree trying to comprehend what's been happening recently. Some very strange things to say the least. First, there was the honey bee that moved across his Peaceful Pluto story as he read it. Then, a bee just happened to land on Tyler's forehead, distracting him. There was no doubt, Tyler would have got the first punch in had he not swiped at it. And then there's Albert. All of a sudden, out of nowhere, this duplicate of himself shows up at his thinking place in the woods, gives him a Shakespeare Ugly Stik as a gift, disappears when his dad appears, leaves it in the oak tree for his dad to find and re-gift for his birthday. Not to mention, the bright beam of light guiding his eyes to the bottom branch of the oak tree ...

"Is everything okay?" Dad asked, poking his head around the door.

"Sure Dad." *Other than the fact that some very strange things have been happening to me in the last little while.*

"Is there anything troubling you?"

"No," he lied. He was having a difficult time trying to figure everything out and until he did, he wanted to keep it to himself.

"You know there's nothing you can't talk to your parents about," his dad smiled, joining him at the window.

He could just imagine talking to his dad about all these strange events. He'd probably tell him what a good story teller he is. "I know Dad."

"It's a beautiful day out there and I have some free time. How about you and I going down to the river to do some serious fishing with that new Shakespeare Ugly Stik of yours?

Jule's Story

"Really!" Jule said, turning quickly to face him.

"Don't look so surprised. I've been meaning to spend some time with you for so long now. Ever since my promotion, I just haven't had the time. But today I do."

"Albert was right! He said one day you won't be too busy."

"Albert?"

"My twin."

"Your imagined twin, Son. Come on. Let's go catch supper."

One day you'll see Dad, he said to himself, as he scooped up the Ugly Stik.

They gathered up their fishing gear while Mom got busy in the kitchen making up a picnic lunch for them. "Just in case you decide to make a day of it," she smiled, handing them the cooler bag.

"Thanks honey. Maybe we will," Dad smiled, winking at Jule.

The sky was a mix of sun and cloud when they left the house. The recent thunderstorm had cooled things down for a few days, but today it was slightly warmer. They chatted back and forth, as they walked along the road to a pathway that led to the river.

"Isn't this where we turn off?" Dad asked, looking toward the worn pathway. The trees seemed so much higher and the brush around them was more overgrown. It saddened him when he realized it had been almost two years since he had walked it. And two years since he'd been fishing with his son.

Jule looked up at his dad who had a strange forlorn look on his face. "We could take this path, but I have a secret fishing place to share with you." His dad sighed and then smiled. "That would be great, Son. Thank you."

They walked a little further down the road then Jule stopped and pointed to a small ledge of slate grey rocks set back a few metres from the side of the road. His dad followed, as they began walking in single file until they came to his thinking place. Dad stood quietly admiring the surroundings. "So this is where you like to spend your time."

"This is only part of it. This area is my thinking place." He was tempted to tell him this was where he came when he skipped school, but decided against it. "No one has ever been here. Except Albert."

His father ignored the part about Albert, concluding that Jule has created an imaginary friend and there was no harm in that. Instead, he stood mesmerized breathing in the fresh pine-scented air, as his eyes scanned the magnificent white pines standing like tall sentries. "I'm honored you have brought me here," he said, after a few minutes.

"Come on. It's this way to the river," Jule said, starting on a dense brush lined path. "If you listen carefully, you will soon begin to hear nature's music," he said, over his shoulder.

As they continued on, the sound of running water, with its soothing melody, became louder with each step. "This is amazing. I didn't even know about this area," his father said, gazing up and down the river, vowing to do this more often. He quickly realized with all work and no play his life was passing by rapidly.

They sat down on a log near the river and cast their lines. Jule sat quietly studying the rod his parents had given him for his birthday. It was identical to the Shakespeare Ugly Stik Albert had given him.

"How's the new rod feel, Son?"

"Good Dad."

"It is the one you wanted, isn't it?"

"Yes. It's identical."

"And what about the No. 10 Hare's Ear Nymph from Kristen?"

"It's identical too."

His dad was puzzled by him saying 'it's identical' and decided it must be some new lingo young people are using. He felt outdated, as it seemed to change constantly.

They sat in the warm sunshine listening to the soothing sound of the river's gentle flow and birds chirping back and forth. It was definitely a perfect day for fishing. Jule looked up in the sky, staring as an osprey circled above. He wondered if it was the same bird that had scooped the fish and flew by him. He looked over at the boulder he had been sitting on when the bird flew by. Even in the warm sun, he felt goose bumps rise on his bare arms thinking about the experience. He was tempted to tell his dad, but decided not to.

"Well, I'm going to reel in and grab some lunch," Dad said after awhile. "The fish just don't seem to be biting. It's probably too late in the morning. How about you, Jule? Would you like to see what Mom has whipped up for us?"

"Sure Dad," he said, reeling in his line and standing the rod up against a poplar tree.

Dad unzipped the cooler bag and reached in for its contents. "Looks like Mom made your favourite sandwich; Salami, old cheddar cheese, lettuce, tomato, hot mustard and mayo."

"On a whole-grain bun," Jule added, as his dad passed him the pale blue, plastic sandwich container.

"You know your mom. She has to get the healthy stuff into us somehow. Here's some celery, carrot and green pepper sticks to go along with it."

They sat side by side on the log eating lunch and watched as a mother deer and her two young fawns came to drink at the river's edge on the opposite side. The identical white spotted twins began frolicking back and forth on shore like two young puppies playing a game of tag.

"No wonder you like to spend so much time here," Dad whispered. "I am definitely going to do this more often. I can't remember when I have felt so relaxed and content."

"Nature will do that for you, Dad. I love spending as much time here as possible," Jule said, placing his empty sandwich container in the cooler bag.

"That sure was a good lunch Mom made for us," Dad said zipping up the bag. "I think we should move downstream and see if we will have better luck there? What do you think?"

Jule looked down the river to where only a few days ago, he had pulled in a four-pound trout with his identical twin, Albert. Though he had enjoyed this time with his dad, he needed to spend some time sorting out everything that had happened recently. "If it's okay with you, Dad, I'd like to go home."

Dad was caught completely off-guard by his request, as he had hoped they could spend the day together. "Sure. That's fine. Are you sure nothing's troubling you?"

There was so much going on in his head, he didn't know what he wanted. He really needed to work through all these recent events that had been happening lately. "I have some homework to do and I'd like to get it done."

Dad's eyes widened. *There's a first. Homework instead of fishing. Something is definitely not right.* He picked up his rod and the cooler bag. "Let's go."

The walk back home was quiet. Dad had to probe for any conversation with Jule, as they made their way through the woods and down the road toward home. When they reached the back door, Jule thanked his dad for going fishing with him and was sorry they got skunked.

"There will be other times, Son. Thanks for taking me to your thinking place."

"You're welcome," he said, heading upstairs to his room.

Dad walked into the great room and sat down beside Mom. "How was the fishing?" she asked, looking up from her magazine.

"No luck. The fish just weren't biting. But that's not all. I'm concerned about Jule. He's been acting strange ever since he opened his gifts this morning. He even asked to come home to do homework."

"Now that's a first," she said, closing the magazine. "Homework instead of fishing?"

"That's what I thought. He's definitely preoccupied about something. I tried to find out what it was, but he didn't seem to want to talk, about anything."

"Well, we both know how he likes to keep to himself."

"I guess. I had a nice time fishing with him this morning. I could have stayed for the day, that's for sure. It was so relaxing connecting with nature. We even saw a mother white tail deer and her two playful fawns drinking at the river's edge, while we ate that delicious lunch you prepared for us. I'd like to spend more time fishing with him."

Jule sat on the edge of his bed and thought about Albert and how much his life had changed since he appeared at his thinking place in the woods. He was positive Albert is real and not someone he had imagined. Still, there was definitely something different about him. He thought of the incident with the bear and how Albert seemed to have full control of it … how he just disappeared when his dad came down the road looking for him. Albert had been right behind him, tying his shoe. Then there was the mysterious bright beam of light shining on the oak tree branch where the Shakespeare Ugly Stik had been left, just before the thunderstorm … how did the rod get there in the first place? At least I know where it is now. He stood the re-gifted rod up against the wall beside his bed. He still couldn't believe his family would do such a thing.

He scooped his *SkyNews* astronomy magazine off the desk then lay down on his bed. As he flipped through the pages he came across an article entitled, "Major Object Discovered Beyond Pluto" and began reading.

6

MONDAY MORNING, JULE waited for his mother's wake-up call. Lately, he had been so preoccupied with Albert and the fishing rod, that he hadn't got around to discussing the wake-up issue with her and again decided to postpone it until the right moment. After she left his room, he slid out of bed and stood at the window watching as a pair of crows walked cautiously out back, searching for nesting materials. He had read in one of his reference books that crows are very particular about what gets used to build their nests. Jule was not surprised that the female had the final say. Even in the bird world, females are the ones in charge. Though he hated to admit it, it made sense, as she is the one spending countless hours hatching the eggs. He watched as the crows began pulling at some long strands of dead grass that surrounded a patch of newer growth. Each crow scooped a mouthful of mud from the mound of dirt that surrounded a mole entry, then flew off into the forest to their nesting area. Crows are territorial and very protective of their young. Though they nest in pairs, distress calls will immediately summon other crows within range. This was proven last summer when eight adult crows chased a black bear out of the woods. As they swooped and squawked, the bear ran as quickly as it could to get away. Crows, being the pack animals they are, were chasing the bear before it could climb the tree and raid their nest.

It was a sunny day and already quite warm. *Another good fishing day*, he sighed, heading toward the bathroom. He was getting anxious for the last day of school.

Jule and Kristen sat across from each other eating breakfast and watched as Mom placed their insulated lunch bags on the side counter. "I have lots of running around to do after my doctor's appointment, but I hope to be home before you get finished school. If not, you both have a key."

"I bet Mom is going to get our special passing into the next grade gift," Kristen whispered to Jule. "I keep giving her hints and I hope she remembers," she said, swallowing the last mouthful of orange juice before taking her dishes to the sink. Last year's hinting was successful, in that, they had both received Nike sport watches for passing. Mom hurried them both along, as she grabbed her purse off the kitchen counter.

"Bye Mom," Kristen said.

"What? No good-bye kiss?"

Kristen quickly ran over to her and kissed her lightly on the cheek.

"I hope you never get too old to kiss and hug your mom."

"Oh Mom," she smiled.

"You too, young man," she said, turning and watching him pick-up his backpack from the kitchen floor. "On Friday, when you left for school, you were nine years old. Now you are ten. It seems like only yesterday that you were my little baby and now you are becoming so grown up."

Bingo! This is a perfect time to talk to her about changing her wake up routine. "Mom, we need to talk."

"What dear?" she said, glancing at the oak pendulum clock on the kitchen wall. "Oh my goodness. I've only got twelve minutes to get to the doctor. Can it wait?" she said, confirming the time with her watch.

"Sure, Mom." They walked out the backdoor and Jule watched as she got into the silver Elantra, wishing he had spoken to her earlier when she came up to wake him. He waved as she drove off, then ran for the bus, with Claire flying after him. Both of them had forgotten to scoop some sunflower seeds. He definitely needed to have a talk with her.

Shortly after he had boarded the bus and sat down at his seat in the back, the snake girl appeared in the aisle. Today, her hair was hanging straight down to her waist with two bright green butterfly clips holding each side in place just above her ears.

"Good morning Jule," Natalie smiled sweetly. "Are you expecting company?" she asked, not waiting for his reply, sitting in the seat beside him. "Isn't it a beautiful day? It's what I call a good fishing day."

"You fish?" Jule said, turning from the window to face her. *The snake girl may have some brains after all.*

"Yes," she smiled. "Why? Do you like fishing?"

"It's my favourite pastime." *That's how I hope to spend all my summer days.*

"That's great! Maybe we could go fishing together over the summer holidays."

"Maybe," he said, turning back to the window. *She's the last person I want to fish with. That would be even worse than fishing with Kristen.* The only girl he had ever fished with was his cousin Pat when they came up from Detroit for a visit. She pulled in the biggest pickerel he had ever seen.

He smiled thinking of how well she could fish, as the bus stopped in front of the school.

"See you again soon," Natalie smiled, before running to meet her friends.

Hopefully never. He waited until she and her friends had started walking down the sidewalk toward the school before hoisting his backpack onto his shoulder and running quickly to the side entrance.

Ms. Annadale gave the kids their work assignments that included 30 minutes of journal writing and completing pages 45 and 46 of their math books. By the time they complete the work it will be recess. The students finally settled down and got to work on their journals and math assignments finishing just before the recess bell sounded. "Hand in your math notebooks please," Ms. Annadale said, over the commotion.

Jule placed his notebook on her desk then scooped his backpack off the hook at the back of the classroom, in case he needed his baseball glove. He walked out the side entrance of the school and put his *Jay's* cap on shielding his eyes from the morning sun, to get a better look at the baseball diamond. He hadn't noticed the kids leaning up against the red brick wall beside the entrance. "Well if it isn't Julie the squealer," Tyler said, still leaning against the wall. Jule knew Tyler's voice so he didn't turn around, instead he proceeded to walk toward the field, ignoring him like his father had suggested.

"Hey, I'm talking to you," he said, walking close behind with his group of friends. Tyler always had to be surrounded by his followers. "What's with the backpack?" he said, pulling hard on the top handle, causing Jule to lose his footing and fall to the ground. "Going somewhere?" The kids began laughing.

"Leave him alone."

Tyler and his friends turned around to see where the voice was coming from.

"Well, if it isn't Julie's big sister defending her little brother."

"I don't need anyone defending me," Jule said, getting to his feet and straightening his backpack.

"Hear that, *Sis*? So why don't you take off?" Tyler said, walking toward Kristen.

Kristen stood her ground. "You are such a jerk Tyler Watson," she said, staring into his blue eyes. "You and your stupid bunch of friends."

He reached out to shove Kristen when a bee landed on his forehead. "What the heck?" He swung at the bee, but it was too late, as he felt its stinger penetrate his skin. "Ow!" he screamed, swinging madly at his forehead trying to brush it off.

"Serves you right," she said, turning on her heel, as her friends starting giggling.

"What are you jerks staring at?" he asked tersely glaring at his friends, as he rubbed his forehead. It was the second time a bee had landed on him. In fact, it was in the exact same spot. "It doesn't even hurt," he lied. It stung like crazy. "Where's that little Julie jerk?" he asked, scanning the area. "I'll deal with that little snitch another time," he said, touching his forehead, as he kept an eye on Kristen. *I'll get you too, sister.*

Kristen spent the remainder of recess looking for Jule, concluding that he probably skipped out again. She was very surprised to see him board the bus back home at the end of the day.

"Where were you all day? I haven't seen you since recess this morning," Kristen said, as they walked to the backdoor.

"I have my places," he smiled, with no intention of telling her. He had spent the remainder of morning recess, lunch hour and afternoon recess in the library. He could tell by the librarian's desk that she was away for the day. In her absence, he was able to do some much needed research about Pluto and beyond. The school library housed many excellent astronomy books and magazines about the universe and with Mrs. Perrin absent, he didn't have to explain why he wasn't outside.

He hung his backpack up at the back door then walked toward the refrigerator. "You didn't have to defend me this morning," he said, pulling out what was left of his birthday cake and placing it on the counter. *It's embarrassing having your older sister fight your battles.*

As usual, his remark put Kristen on the defense. "Maybe, just maybe, I didn't want you sitting outside the principal's office once again. Besides, all your shenanigans come back to haunt me, little brother."

"Can I help it if Tyler is a jerk?"

"Yeah. A jerk who's after your butt. He got his after you took off. He got stung by a bee and walked around with a big red lump in the middle of his forehead for the rest of the day."

"I can handle him," Jule said, cutting a piece of cake then licking the icing off the knife. "Wait a minute. What did you say?"

"If you weren't so busy stuffing your face, you would have heard me. I said, Tyler got his when a bee stung him on the forehead."

Jule stood staring at Kristen. That was the second time a bee had landed on Tyler's forehead. It's like the first time was a warning.

"What Jule? You look so stunned."

"It's nothing," he said, wrapping up the cake and putting it back in the fridge.

"Did you wash your hands, Jule Desjoux? Just because Mom isn't here."

"I will," he said, shutting the refrigerator door. He was definitely getting sick of females trying to run his life.

"Well!" she persisted.

"You aren't my mother!" he yelled, walking into the bathroom beside the kitchen and slamming the door.

Mom and Dad arrived home at the same time and prepared dinner together, as they talked about their day. When they sat down to dinner Mom asked how their day went. As usual, Jule had very little to say. All he wanted to do was finish dinner so he could get to his room and go over the notes he had gathered about Pluto and the universe beyond. Kristen complained about her workload and how she could hardly wait for the school year to be over, as she really needed a break. "Guess what else happened?" Kristen said, putting her fork down on the plate.

Jule took a mouthful of mashed potato from his plate and began chewing it as if it were a thick piece of steak, as he looked across the table at his sister. *Here we go*, he thought miserably.

"I had to deal with Tyler Watson today."

"The Tyler Watson that Jule ..."

"... punched in the face," Kristen continued, finishing her mother's sentence. "Yeah, that jerk."

"Kristen, I have asked you not to talk that way."

"I'm only telling the truth, Mom. He is a total idiot. Anyway, he tried to cheat on the math test we had after recess this morning by looking at my paper. So, I let him. But stupid Tyler didn't know that I put down all incorrect answers."

Jule stopped chewing his potatoes and swallowed. *How cool is this?* He couldn't wait to hear what happened next.

"What about your test?" Dad asked, taking a sip of wine.

"After stupid Tyler copied all my wrong answers and handed it into the teacher, I filled in the correct answers on my good copy from the back of the rough copy that I let him see. He was so proud of himself because he was the first one to finish," she chuckled. "After he handed in his test, he sat there with a swollen forehead grinning from ear to ear."

Jule thought of Tyler with his swollen forehead. *Maybe Kristen isn't so bad after all.* He would wait until after dinner to congratulate her though.

"Weren't you worried about running out of time?"

One thing about Kristen, she was very sure of herself. "Mom. I am the best math student in my class. Why do you think he copied MY work? But, here's the best part. Mr. Banks said I was the only student who got a perfect score! You should have seen the look on Tyler's face!"

Jule couldn't hold back any longer. "Yes!" he yelled, raising his arm and pulling it back down to his side. "Yes! Yes! Yes! Good going Kristen!"

Mom and Dad watched the two of them banter back and forth then Dad cut in and made a suggestion. "Maybe next time you should just cover your work so he can't see it. After all, you don't want to risk losing your first place status."

"That will never happen," Kristen said, excusing herself from the table.

Jule smiled as he thought about the look on Tyler's face. *Serves him right. Sometimes, she can be a great sister.* He excused himself from the table and took his plate over to the sink.

As soon as he left the kitchen, Mom leaned over the table. "Jule seemed more like himself tonight," she whispered.

Jule's Story

Dad didn't agree. Though he was more talkative, he was only supporting his sister against Tyler. It seemed he wasn't well liked by either of them. "Jule is still not himself and it all seemed to start on his birthday after he opened up the Shakespeare Ugly Stik we gave him. From that point on, it's like he's off in another world somewhere. Something has definitely got him preoccupied."

"I guess. Something or someone. And he doesn't want to talk about it," Mom said, removing the remaining dishes from the table. She had noticed a change in him lately and was hoping it was just the normal adolescent changes a young boy experiences at this age.

Jule stared out his bedroom window watching as daylight faded to night. His research in the library today confirmed that there is a mysterious planet-like body, three-quarters the size of Pluto, that has been discovered orbiting the sun, in a huge elliptical path well beyond Pluto's orbit. He wasn't sure why this information was significant, but something in the back of his mind kept telling him somehow, it may be connected to Albert. He closed the curtains and sat down at his desk then began reading his Peaceful Pluto story. He finished the first paragraph then sat back heavily in his chair. He still believed that Pluto should remain one of the nine planets, especially now that there could be a tenth planet that astronomers and scientists don't know existed. He leaned forward to continue reading his story. There was a honey bee standing patiently under the first word of the second paragraph. Jule stared down at the tiny creature wondering where it came from. He remembered what had occurred in class when he read his story to his classmates. He began reading the first sentence very slowly. *Peaceful Pluto is a place where man has not interfered.* Sure enough, the bee kept pace with each word he read. He read the next sentence, only this time, as quickly as he could. *Therefore, birds of many shades of orange, lime, fuchsia, mauve, yellow, and turquoise fly freely throughout trees that never die.* Jule was astounded. The bee had kept pace with each word. This was no longer a coincidence and he wondered what to do. He didn't want to kill the bee. And he certainly couldn't touch it because it could sting him. He decided to show Kristen the word bee. It took a little explaining and coaxing, but Kristen being his nosy sister, accompanied him back to his room. "You've heard of spelling bees, well this is a word bee," Jule chuckled, as they entered his room.

Kristen was not impressed. "This had better be good," she said, peering down at the paper on his desk. "I don't see a bee. Where's this stupid bee, Jule?" Sure enough it was gone.

"That can't be, pardon the pun. No really! It was sitting right under the word die!"

"That's what's going happen to you if you keep bugging me," Kristen said, turning on her heel and leaving his room. She had little patience for anything these days.

Oh man. What the heck is going on? It was right here on my story. He figured it must have flown off when they came into the room, so he began looking around to see if he could find it. He shook the curtains and watched to see if it flew off. Then he examined all around the window. He cleared his desk off and picked up his dirty clothes, but the bee was nowhere in sight. Once again, he thought of Albert and sensed he had something to do with all the coincidences that continued to happen in his life. But, was Albert real and the missing link to all his questions? Or did he imagine him like Dad said? *He is definitely real and so is the Shakespeare Ugly Stik that he gave me that day when I caught the trout.* He sat on the edge of his bed examining the rod and finally solved the mystery around it. He was never supposed to retrieve the

Jule's Story

rod on the night of the storm. Albert had left it in the tree for his parents to find and give to him for his birthday. That way, he wouldn't have to explain Albert's gift. Although the rod dilemma was solved, what about Albert? *Where is he? This is all so strange. If only I could meet with Albert just one more time. Then maybe I could get to the bottom of all this.*

Jule washed and got ready for bed then crawled under the navy comforter and quickly fell into a deep sleep. On the ceiling above him, the bee moved slowly across the galaxy posters, resting on a small land mass, just beyond Pluto.

7

THE SCHOOL YEAR was almost over and Jule still hadn't talked to his mom about waking up with the clock radio. He listened for her approaching footsteps and decided now was as good a time as any.

"Good morning," she said, heading for the window.

"Morning, Mom." He watched her pull open the curtains and stare out the window for a moment. She seemed to enjoy staring out back, as this was also part of her routine. As he lay in bed watching her, he wondered if he should say anything. He decided to proceed, as he really wanted to get up on his own. He had thought about the best approach for many days now and finally decided the best way of handling this delicate situation. "Mom."

"Yes dear," she smiled, turning away from the window. He loved seeing her smile first thing in the morning. This is going to be more difficult than he imagined, but he proceeded. "How old was Kristen when she started using her clock radio for getting up in the morning?"

Mom thought about how long ago it had been. "I think she was about your age, maybe younger." Kristen had become very independent of her parents at an early age. "Why?" she asked, sitting down on the edge of the bed. Jule had hoped she would see the connection, but it seemed to go over her head. He sat up in bed to make his point. "Because I think I'm old enough now to start using my radio alarm." There it was out. He watched intently for her reaction.

"In other words, you really don't need your mom coming upstairs every morning and waking you up for school," she sighed. *How dumb am I?* she thought. *Maybe this is why he has been acting so strange lately. I have been treating him like a young child instead of a maturing young lad.* "You are so right, sweetheart," she smiled. "From now on, you can wake-up on your own."

Jule's eyes widened. It hadn't been difficult after all. In fact, she was totally happy with his request. There was no guilt trip. No objection. Nothing. He wished he had done it sooner.

"But if you oversleep, I'll come up and wake you."

He figured there was a catch. But he could live with that. He would be up and dressed long before she would have to. "And another thing," he continued, seeing he was on a roll. "I would like to start making my own breakfast choices."

"Sounds good to me," Mom said, walking out of the room. She stopped and stuck her head around the bedroom door. "As long as it's healthy," she smiled, before closing it. Mom could hardly wait to tell Dad that this is the reason Jule has been acting so strangely lately. All he needed was his independence.

This is the best morning I've had in a long time. I finally get to wake up with the radio. He flicked it on and listened as Bon Jovi's, 'It's My Life' filled the room. He set the alarm then jumped out of bed to look at the calendar. Only a few more weeks until summer holidays. Jule counted the days, as he put on his raglan sleeved navy athletic top and long beige twill shorts. He reached in his drawer for a clean hankie. He was the only kid who carried one. He asked his friend Andrew if he had one and he looked at him like he was from another planet. Mom insisted on this ancient practice and said that grandpa Albert always had one tucked in his pocket in case he had to blow his nose. Jule had argued that there are tissues for nose blowing now and had refused to carry one. She said it may come in handy one day, and then she showed him how to make a bandana with just a few folds. He really liked that idea. He often whipped one up to tie around his head to keep the sweat out of his eyes when he was out for his long runs. Though he never used it for nose blowing, he did find it came in handy for wiping his face or wetting with cold water and putting on his forehead whenever he was hot. He was so used to carrying one now, that he could not imagine life without it. He tucked it into his back pocket. He stood by his open bedroom window and watched as a male ruby-throat hummingbird defended its territory. *Stupid crow.* He figured it must be a young, inexperienced bird, as it clumsily flew up then down in the sky trying to avoid the angry hummer with its piercing beak. Jule watched as it swooped and poked at the crow until it was out of his area. A male humming bird protecting his nesting territory will take on anything who dares enter into it, including a hungry crow looking for eggs or newly hatched nestlings.

Jule walked into the sunny kitchen and was surprised to find it vacant. He figured Mom would be hanging around making sure that he made a wise breakfast choice. They had finished off the last of his birthday cake at dinner last night, so that was out. He pulled a loaf of bread out of the freezer and read the wrapper. Then he went to the cupboard and pulled out the bran flakes box. It was very difficult not to make a nutritional choice, as everything was prefaced with 100% whole grain. He decided on a couple of slices of toast topped off with thickly spread peanut butter and homemade strawberry jam that ran off the sides of his toast with every bite. He was just finishing off his glass of apple juice when Mom and Kristen entered the kitchen.

"Not much longer before summer vacation begins," Mom said, placing two thermal lunch bags on the counter. Jule could hardly wait. "Nothing but fishing and more fishing," he smiled, wiping his face with a napkin.

"Don't you think of anything else but fishing?" Kristen asked, looking toward the kitchen ceiling. She was probably still miffed about last night's fiasco with the honey bee.

"Eating!" he said, throwing in the last mouthful of toast, as he scooped his backpack up onto his shoulder.

"Enjoy your day kids," Mom said, scooping out some sunflower seeds. "Here. You can start doing this." She handed Jule the plastic scoop.

"Sure," Jule said, reaching in the large container for a handful. *Who needs a scoop?* "Have a good day, Mom." Feeling totally independent, he ran toward the bus stop whistling for Claire, waiting patiently for her arrival. Lately he wondered where she was, as she often missed her morning feeding. He concluded it must be nesting time. He smiled, as Claire and her mate landed on the edge of his open hand. "Hey Kristen, do you want some sunflower seeds?" He already knew the answer.

"No, I don't want some sunflower seeds. It's bad enough that you stand out here every morning making a jerk out of yourself."

"I wouldn't say that," he smiled, as chickadees continued landing on his head, shoulders and arms waiting for a turn. "It really feels good connecting with nature."

"I'm sure," she snarled, as the bus approached.

Jule watched as Claire flew off with the last seed before boarding the bus. He sat down at the back feeling the bright sunshine on his face through the open window. *I can hardly wait for summer holidays to begin ...*

"Morning Jule," Natalie said, sitting down beside him. Today, her long, thick, brown snake hung over her left shoulder. He edged himself closer to the window. "Do you have any plans for summer vacation?" she continued.

"Fishing." *And more fishing.* But he wasn't going to tell her how much. He continued staring out the window. He didn't want to miss his favourite rock face, again. *The snake girl is always in my face* he sighed leaning hard into the side of the bus.

"We are going whale watching off the coast of Labrador for three weeks in July."

"Whale watching! That would be really neat," Jule said, turning to face her.

"I will take lots of pictures and show you, if you like?"

Though he would like to see the pictures, he didn't tell her that. Instead he turned back to the window. She must think he was awfully rude, but it was the only way he could think of to discourage her.

"Maybe we could go fishing some time during our vacation," she smiled sweetly. "When I get back."

"Maybe." As soon as the word was out of his mouth, he realized he had made a big mistake giving her any hope.

"Shall I give you my phone number so you can call me to arrange a day?"

One thing about the snake girl, she's persistent. "Whatever." *It doesn't mean I'm going to call you. In fact, don't count on it.*

Natalie quickly jotted down her phone number with a bright red marker. "Here Jule. Don't hesitate to call me."

Without looking at it, he tucked the neatly folded piece of paper in the left pocket of his navy shirt and never gave it another thought. The bus ride seemed to take much longer today, and he had never been more thankful to see the school in his life.

As the kids disembarked, Jule sat by the open window and watched as Natalie got off the bus and walked toward her girlfriends who were waiting for her on the sidewalk. "Jule and I are going fishing this summer!" Natalie said excitedly.

"You are?" they said in unison. They all knew how much she liked him. He was all she ever talked about. "Yes! I gave him my phone number and he is going to call me to arrange a date! I think he really likes me. He is so cute. I hope he's in my class next year." She was so glad she had persevered. Now they are going fishing together and she could hardly wait.

Great. Now the snake girl thinks I like her. He remained on the bus watching as Natalie and her friends walked toward the school, then ran as fast as he could for the side entrance and into his classroom, as the bell sounded for classes to begin.

The teacher gave them their last writing assignment for the year, with summer as its theme. "I want you to tell me what you would like to do on your holiday? What your ideal day is? Who you would like to spend some time with?" They had until recess to write their stories. "Don't forget your dictionaries!"

Jule began writing his story. 'This summer I hope to do lots of fishing with Albert, my twin. He gave me a Shakespeare Ugly Stik for my birthday, even though it wasn't my birthday yet.' He continued writing until Ms. Annadale announced it was getting near recess. When the bell sounded she stood by the classroom door to collect the stories. Jule finished the last sentence then handed it the teacher who glanced down at the first line and read it. "I didn't know you had a twin."

"I do. My mom said 'everyone has a twin'. Even you Ms. Annadale," Jule said, hoisting his backpack onto his shoulder and walking away. His teacher continued reading the story as she walked toward her desk.

Though the skies had been nice and clear this morning, the sun was playing hide and seek with clouds that dotted the sky. Jule looked around for Andrew and his team mates. It had been days since he played baseball. He heard Andrew calling his name and stopped to wave as he ran toward the baseball diamond. Jule ran quickly and caught up with him. "Man you can run fast," Andrew panted, as they both slowed to a walk. "You should try out for the Olympics or something."

Jule often dreamt of competing in the Olympics one day. He really loved to run. Not only did it keep him lean and muscular, but it cleared his head when life got too stressed. He hoped one day, to put his whole mind and body into the constant training it would take to even think about entering the Olympics. "Come on," he said, pulling Andrew's white jersey. "There's only a few more days to beat Bozo Barrett and the gang."

"I can't keep up with you," Andrew called, as Jule ran ahead. When he finally arrived at the diamond, he quickly walked over to where the teams were being chosen and stood beside Jule.

They were just about to choose teams, when Tyler decided it was time to be annoying.

"Hey Julie. What's that hanging out of your back pocket?"

Jule chose to ignore him, but not before he told Tyler the correct pronunciation of his name.

"Okay Jule. What's that thing?" Tyler asked, moving up closer behind him for a better look. "Yuk! It looks like a dirty old hankie to me," he said, as Jule reached behind, tucking it into his pocket. "That's disgusting. It's probably full of snot," Tyler said, making a face. "Isn't using a hankie a little outdated? No one carries one anymore. At least no one I know. Of course with a name like Julie ..."

"Okay Tyler. Knock it off," Barrett cut in. "I'm picking the teams today," he continued.

"You always pick the teams," Andrew said sarcastically.

"Yeah I do," he said, turning toward him. "And it's a sure bet you won't be on it."

"Who'd want to be on your stupid team anyway?" he mumbled, pushing the dirt around with his foot.

"You would you little jerk."

Danny looked at his watch. "Can we get going and pick the teams?" Had he not interfered, the incessant banter would have continued and there would be no time to play.

"Sure," Barrett said. He turned toward Jule and smiled. "Today, I am going to give you the privilege of being on my team." Next to himself, he knew Jule was one of the best players in the school.

Jule was surprised that Barrett wanted him on his team. It was just a few days ago that he was part of the Tyler antagonists. He said he wanted to be on the same team as Andrew.

Barrett walked over to where he stood. "Do you realize what an honor it is to be picked for my team?"

"Somehow, I just don't feel worthy," Jule said sarcastically.

"That was your last chance. I'm never asking you again."

Jule's Story

The truth was, he would never be on his team.

The teams were decided and as usual, Barrett's team won the toss and it didn't take long for them to be up three runs. When the opposing team was up to bat, Tyler made sure Jule was aware of what the score was when he took his place at home plate.

"Stand back everybody. Julie is trying for a home run," Tyler said, tossing the ball in the air a few times. "Besides, your team only has one player on base so even if you do connect, we'll still be the winners."

"Just pitch it," Jule yelled. Tyler looked straight at him and fired a hard right that connected with Jule's metal bat sending the ball high above Tyler's head. He dropped the bat and ran quickly to first then toward second. He turned and watched as Barrett ran after the fly ball.

"Mine," he yelled, trying to keep up with it. The teams watched as Barrett fell to the ground and the ball sailed over him.

Tyler kicked at the dirt around the pitcher's mound as Jule's team cheered him home. "Hey Barrett," he yelled, not turning around to look. "I think you missed it, stupid jerk," he muttered.

As Jule crossed home plate, he turned to see what was happening in left field. Barrett had missed the ball and was laying face down in the grass. His team continued to call him, but there was no response. Sensing there was something wrong, Jule ran out to the field to Barrett. His team mates followed, then the remainder of Barrett's team. By the time they arrived, Jule was on his knees beside Barrett trying to get a response.

"Barrett. Can you hear me?"

After a few seconds, he finally responded. "What happened?" he asked, groggily.

"You took a tumble," Jule said, turning to one of his team mates. "Glenn, run into the school and tell them to dial 911, then report back to me." Glenn turned and started running for the school. Jule was thankful he had spent a week of his vacation last summer taking a St. John Ambulance course. At the time, he didn't want to give up his precious fishing time, but now he witnessed firsthand how beneficial the course is. The other kids didn't know what to do. He remembered the necessary steps to take. The first was to assess the situation, making sure he himself was in no danger. The next step was to assess the patient. Is he conscious? Next, if possible, send someone to get help and very importantly, make sure they come back and report that they followed through with your request.

"Barrett."

"Yes," he said, opening his eyes. He was still laying face down in the dirt, but had moved his head enough to reveal a large gash on his forehead that was bleeding.

"Does it hurt to move?" Jule asked, beginning to examine him from head to toe for broken bones.

"Just my head is pounding." Barrett managed to flip himself over onto his back, which was a good sign, as there seemed to be no broken bones. Jule reached into his pocket for some folded tissues and his hankie. He could hear his mom's voice saying *you never know when you will need it*. He was really glad he had shoved a clean one in his back pocket this morning.

He called Danny over, and asked him to kneel behind Barrett and place his hands on either side of his head to steady it. Fortunately, he didn't seem to be upset with the sight of blood, as some of the others would have nothing to do with it.

Jule's Story

Breathlessly, Glenn reported back to Jule that Mr. Coulter called for an ambulance and that he is on his way. "Thanks Glenn. Did you hear that?" Jule said, continuing to make sure Barrett remained conscious.

"Yup."

"You have a wound on your forehead that needs tending to."

"I do? Does it make me look ugly?" He thought of Tamara that sat across from him in class. He really liked her and hoped she liked him too.

"Nah. It shows you're a rough and tumble kinda guy. I'm going to cover the wound. I'll try not to hurt you," Jule said, cleaning away some of the loose dirt with a clean tissue. Thankfully, the bleeding had stopped, but there was quite a gash, he observed. Meticulously, he folded the remaining clean tissues and placed them on the cut. He instructed Danny to gently hold them there while he placed his hankie on Barrett's tummy and folded it into a triangle. The kids stood by and watched. He started at the point and began folding it into pleats like an accordion until a bandana had formed. Gently, he placed it over the stacked tissues, and then secured it at the back of Barrett's head. *That should do it.* "How do you feel?"

"I'm okay," he said, trying to sit up.

"Don't try to get up, Barrett. Just lay still. Help is on the way," Jule said, not leaving his side.

Mr. Coulter arrived at the same time as the ambulance. He put his arms up as a barrier to keep the kids back. "Stand back everyone. Let the paramedics do their job."

Jule stood up and moved away from Barrett, as the paramedics wheeled the stretcher beside him.

"How are you doing, son?" a paramedic asked.

"I'm okay. Just a little dizzy. And my head hurts," he added, pointing to the bandage.

The kids watched as the paramedics did a routine check on Barrett. "BP is normal. Pulse normal," one said to the other, as he continued examining Barrett from head to toe. "We're going to take you to the hospital so the doctor can take a look at that wound," he said reassuringly, as they lifted him onto the stretcher.

"Wow! I've never ridden in an ambulance before," Barrett beamed. "Can we put the siren on?"

"Sure son," the paramedic smiled.

Mr. Coulter approached one of the paramedics and introduced himself. "How's he doing?" he asked, with a concerned look.

"I'm quite sure he is going to be fine. He may need a couple of stitches on his forehead. Please contact the parents and have them meet him at the hospital," he said, opening the passenger door. "Oh, there's one other thing," he said, before climbing inside. "Whoever was first on the scene handled it like a pro. Made our job a whole lot easier."

"Thanks," Mr. Coulter said proudly wondering who it was.

The kids watched as the ambulance approached the school driveway. The siren sounded and the lights started flashing, as it exited onto the road. The kids all cheered and waved.

"Looks like Barrett got his wish," Tyler said, as his team stood and watch it drive out of sight.

The kids began walking toward the school with Mr. Coulter leading the way.

"I guess that dirty old hankie of yours had some use after all," Tyler said, turning to Jule.

Jule's Story

He just smiled as he picked up his backpack. He couldn't help notice that the bee sting in the middle of Tyler's forehead was still a bright fuscia.

At the end of the school day, Mr. Coulter announced on the PA that Barrett was examined at the hospital and needed a few stitches, and then he went home with his parents.

At supper that night, Kristen couldn't wait to tell her parents about the accident. "Something awful happened at school today. Barrett, he's my classmate, was running for a fly ball when he must have hit a rabbit hole or something and fell headfirst to the ground splitting his head open on a rock. It was so bad, the paramedics came to the school."

"Oh my goodness," mom said. "I hope he's okay."

"He is. Barrett just needed a few stitches. The principal announced it at the end of the day."

"Did you see it happen, Jule?" Dad asked.

Jule looked up from his dinner. He wanted to tell them what exactly had happened but decided not to. "It was my home run."

"It figures you would be in there somewhere," Kristen said emphatically. Thank goodness, the knock at the side door interrupted her rant.

"I'll get it," Dad said, wondering who it could be?

"Hello Mr. Desjoux. My name is Barrett and these are my parents."

"Doug Higgins. This is my wife, Pat," his father said, putting his hand out.

"Ross," Dad said, wiping his hand on his jeans before shaking Doug's outstretched hand.

"Sorry to bother you. I would like to return Jule's hankie," Barrett smiled. "Thanks to him, I'll be just fine."

Ross looked at the small clean bandage on Barrett's forehead and quickly realized this was the kid Kristen spoke of at the dinner table. He wondered what role Jule's hankie had played. "Please, come in. He's in the kitchen," he said, leading them through a small hallway.

They all looked toward the Higgins as they entered the kitchen. Kristen was first to speak. "Barrett?"

He could tell by the questioning look on her face that he was the last person she expected to see in the kitchen. "It's me, Kristen. But it's not you I came to see," he said, walking toward Jule. "I came to thank you for what you did today," Barrett said sincerely. "If it weren't for you, I'd probably still be laying face down in the field. Here's your hankie back and a package of new ones," he smiled, handing them to him.

Jule looked down at the laundered, pressed hankie and the package of new ones. "Thanks."

"No, thank you son," Mr. Higgins said. "Barrett told us what you did and we are all very grateful. You folks should be very proud of him," he smiled.

"We are," Dad said, with a surprised look. He introduced the Higgins to his wife, Laura, as the kids chatted at the table.

"We'd better not keep you folks any longer," Mr. Higgins said. "Sorry about interrupting your dinner, but we wanted to come over and express our gratitude."

"Hey, this is one interruption we don't mind at all," Mom smiled, looking over at Jule. "Would you like to stay for coffee and dessert?"

"No, thanks. We have to get Barrett back home so he's ready for school tomorrow."

"Aw Dad, do I have to go?" he said, getting up from the table.

"You know what the doctor said. You are to carry on as usual," Mr. Higgins smiled.

"See you tomorrow, Jule. You too, Kristen. And thanks again," he smiled, raising his hand.

Dad showed them to the door then sat back down at the table. Before he could congratulate Jule, Kristen was already in the driver's seat. "So you're the student! The principal was asking all the kids who had performed the first aid before the paramedics arrived and no one seemed to know. Stupid Tyler said he did it. Needless to say, no one believed him, including Mr. Coulter. Even he knew Tyler's totally incapable." Jule wondered why none of the kids told the principal he had performed first aid. Then again, if he had asked Tyler and his dumb friends, it was no wonder they didn't mention him.

Everyone, including Kristen, sat quietly and listened as Jule told them the real story of what happened in the field this afternoon.

"Wow! I am really proud of you, Son. I guess that St. John Ambulance course you took at Fleming College last summer paid off," Dad beamed.

"I am proud of you too," Mom smiled.

"I can just see the look on Tyler's face and his stupid friends' faces when they find out," Kristen said. "Imagine, my brother, the school hero."

Tyler and his friends already knew and Jule was not surprised they didn't tell Mr. Coulter. He excused himself from the table and went up to his room.

He stood by his bedroom window and watched as a chipmunk scrounged the ground for seeds under the empty bird feeder, that may have been missed by the birds during the winter months. The feeder would remain empty until late fall. Filling them at this time of year would only be asking for trouble, as hungry bears would destroy the feeder to get at the seeds. He was surprised that his parents hadn't brought it in. There was no sense tempting the bears. He thought about the bear that Albert had sent running off into the bush. Then his thoughts turned to the Shakespeare Ugly Stik he had given him. Since then, he had only used it to fish on his birthday with his dad. For whatever reason, his parents re-gifting of the rod had put a damper on his enjoyment. Hopefully, that will change as there will be lots of time once summer holidays begin.

The next day, the principal called Ms. Annadale over the P.A. asking her to send Jule down to the office. She already knew the reason and before he left the room, she told him how proud she was. Word was out all over the school, that Jule Desjoux was the student who first attended Barrett.

Jule entered the main office where the secretary congratulated him, and then sent him into Mr. Coulter's office. The principal congratulated him and told him that he would be given a special award at the awards assembly this evening for the way he took complete charge of the accident scene. "It took me awhile to find out who the student was. I had assumed that it was one of our senior students in grade seven or eight. Needless to say, when I discovered that it was a grade four student, I was thrilled. Your teammate, Glenn came to the office first thing this morning and told me how you had taken charge of the situation. I am very proud you are one of our students, Jule."

Jule wasn't sure what all the fuss was about and certainly didn't think of himself as a hero. His knowledge of what to do in such a situation was a direct result of the St. John Ambulance course he'd taken last summer. He had enjoyed the course so much that he was considering becoming a paramedic one day.

Jule's Story

    At seven that evening, the students and parents filed into the school auditorium for the end of the year awards assembly. Jule received an award for track and field and honor student. Kristen scored one for honor student also. After all the awards had been presented, the principal made his way to the podium to congratulate all the student achievements. "This has been one of the longest awards assembly I have ever had the honor of attending. Once again, I am very proud of all the students of J. D. Hodgson." He waited for the applause to stop then continued. "Now, if you can just bear with me for a few more moments, there is one last award to be given out. I am sure by now, most of you have heard about the accident yesterday involving one of our students. I am happy to say that the student, Barrett Higgins, is fine, thanks to the skillful way the situation was handled by another student, Jule Desjoux. Not only did Jule react calmly and sensibly, but he took complete charge of what could have been a very serious situation. Before the paramedics arrived, Jule had performed first aid and did such a good, thorough job they recommended he be given a special award. Jule, will you please come up here?"

    The audience clapped and some cheered, as he made his way to the front of the auditorium. The two paramedics who attended the scene had joined the principal. "Jule," the paramedic began, "on behalf of Barrett, his family, the students, parents, teachers and paramedics, we present you with this award." He handed him an engraved wooden plaque and an envelope. "Keep up the good work son," he smiled and shook Jule's hand as cameras flashed. Jule shook hands with the principal and second paramedic, as the audience rose in a standing ovation. He asked the principal if he could say a few words. The principal nodded and put his hands up to silence the crowd. "Thank you for this award," he said humbly. "I credit the skills I learned from enrolling in a St. John Ambulance course and highly recommend it to everyone."

"Good advice Jule, thank you. That concludes our awards assembly folks," the principal waved. "Parents, thank you for showing your support, once again. Have a great summer."

Jule remained up front with the principal and paramedics, as the people exited.

"We are so proud of you," Mom said, hugging him tightly when she reached the front of the auditorium. His parents shook hands with the principal and paramedics then joined the moving crowd. They chatted back and forth as they walked to their burgundy Subaru SUV parked in the rear parking lot of the school. He showed his parents and Kristen the plaque engraved with his name and the accompanying gift certificate for Master's Book Store in the village.

"We were so proud of you, son," Dad said, starting the car.

"Me too little brother. Imagine, my own little brother the hero of the school," Kristen sighed, pleasantly waving to her friends from the backseat as they exited the parking lot, definitely loving the celebrity status surrounding her. After all, she was his sister.

Jule found the whole experience quite overwhelming and would have preferred that the incident hadn't happened in the first place. He was leery of everyone being so nice and wondered how long it would last. Even Tyler was on his best behaviour, and shook his hand as his parents looked on. As they entered Tim Horton's parking lot, his thoughts turned to the white icing, maple-caramel donut and chocolate milk he was going to order.

8

JULE TURNED OVER onto his side when the clock radio sounded at eight. *Only two more days left of school.* He could hardly wait, as he threw back the covers and started to dress. He picked his navy shirt off the floor and remembered spilling chocolate milk on the front of it last night, so he chucked it into the clothes hamper. He put on the clean beige shirt he had worn the day Albert appeared at his thinking place. He was beginning to wonder if Albert was just a figment of his imagination, as he hadn't seen him since. There was also the mystery of an osprey hovering above him in the sky whenever he fished by the river. Though he remained elusive Jule had a gut feeling that Albert, the osprey, and even the honey bee were connected in some way. He just wasn't sure how.

Jule quickly finished his bowl of *Raisin Bran* then ran for the school bus as it pulled up in front of the house. He had spent so much time thinking about Albert that he was almost late for it. He quickly walked toward the back of the bus and sat in his usual seat by the window. The bus was emptier, as some of the students who were going away for vacation had been lucky enough to miss the last two days of school. Unfortunately, Natalie wasn't one of them.

"Good morning Jule," she smiled sweetly before sitting down beside him. Her thick brown snake was divided into two thinner snakes that stuck out both sides of her head. She reminded him of Andrew's cocker spaniel, Sammy, with its big, floppy, droopy, brown ears. "I think that what you did for Barrett is really neat," she began.

"It was nothing," Jule said, continuing to stare out the window. He had hoped all this hero stuff was finally in the past.

"Well, I think it was wonderful. You are the school hero." She sat quietly for a few minutes then told him that she wouldn't be on the bus tomorrow because they were leaving for the coast. *What a shame! Finally peace and quiet, even if it's only for a day.* Jule could hardly wait. He watched as the bus pulled up in front of the school opening its doors for the students to disembark. "I hope you will call me to go fishing," she sang out, before exiting the bus.

Great! Now everybody will know, he sighed before leaving his seat.

"Hope you call me to go fishing," Kristen mimicked, as Jule got off the bus.

"Put a sock in it Kristen," he said angrily, before running to the side entrance.

After the bell rang, the students reluctantly took their seats. Knowing there was only two days remaining, Ms. Annadale gave the kids the option of reading, writing, doing art work or, a rapid math contest. The kids all cheered in unison for the math contest. It was a great way for the students to improve their math skills. She lined up the girls on one side of the room and the boys on the other. It's a simple game where the teacher calls out a math problem and

Jule's Story

allots a team ten seconds to answer. If they answer incorrectly or don't answer in time, the opposing team gets a chance at the question. So, it is imperative that everyone pay attention.

"When you know the answer, raise your hand. The boys won the toss so we will begin on their side. What's sixteen times seven?"

Brian quickly raised his hand. "110."

"Incorrect. Lindsay?"

"112."

"Correct."

"What's twenty-four times 10?" "Caitlin?"

"240."

"Correct." The students were having so much fun, they continued playing the math quiz until the recess bell sounded. Ms. Annadale read the scores out, giving the highest score last.

"Boys 115, girls 117." The girls caught on immediately, as the boys began cheering. The girls stood quietly and waited for one of them to figure it out. Finally, Craig said reluctantly that the girls were the winners. They had learned yet another valuable lesson and that was to listen carefully. The girls began cheering and chanting that they rule, as they left the classroom for recess. Ms. Annadale stood at the open doorway smiling as they walked out. She was going to miss this class. They were all good students.

Jule looked toward the field to see if a final baseball game had been organized. He put his hand on his forehead to shield his eyes from the bright sunshine because he had forgotten his hat. In the meantime, some kids he didn't know walked up to congratulate him on his award.

"I guess you think you're a big hot shot now," Tyler said, sauntering up beside him.

As he had suspected, Jule quickly realized that Tyler had been putting on a big show for the parents last night. "Knock it off, Tyler." Everyone, including Jule turned to see where the voice was coming from.

Tyler walked toward Barrett. "Don't tell me you are taking Julie's side just because he put a little bandage on your head."

"I don't need anybody taking my side," Jule said defensively.

Tyler turned back toward him. "I could clean your clock."

"And I could clean yours," Jule retorted, watching as a bee began circling around Tyler's head.

Tyler was just about to shove Jule when Barrett stepped in sending Tyler sprawling to the ground. "I said knock it off," Barrett yelled.

Tyler who had fallen down on his butt, quickly got to his feet. "Hey man. I'm your buddy, remember," he said, standing tall. Just then, the bee that had landed on his forehead flew off. Not missing a beat, Tyler turned and watched as Jule ran toward the field. "Julie, Julie, Julie," he began chanting. "Look at that little jerk go," he laughed.

"You're the jerk Tyler. Even a bee won't hang around you. I can't believe we were ever friends," Barrett said, before walking away.

"Yeah, well I wouldn't want you for a friend anyway," Tyler yelled. "Go be friends with Julie. See if I care." Tyler thought back to the confrontation with Jule and remembered seeing a bee circling his head, but he didn't feel it land. He touched his forehead. The bee sting was almost healed but for some reason it began throbbing like crazy as he watched Jule run quickly across the field, and off the school grounds.

Jule took some short cuts and continued running until he reached his thinking place in the woods. He sat down on a log to catch his breath and pulled out his hankie, which he had forgotten was full of sunflower seeds, that now lay scattered on the ground. He wiped the perspiration off his face then tied the hankie into a bandana. Soon the chickadees, appeared on nearby branches. He watched as they scoured the ground around his feet for the fallen seeds and began telling them about his lousy morning recess. He didn't want to go back to school so he made his way down to the river and sat on his favourite log thinking about his fishing experience with Albert.

'This must be a four pounder. I have never been this lucky." And he hadn't been since. He looked up into the clear sky. *The osprey must be somewhere else*, he concluded when it was nowhere in sight. He was beginning to think that Albert was someone he had imagined. Jule turned and looked down the river to where he had fished with Albert then abruptly stood up to take a better look at the distant figure fishing down river. *It can't be!* He began running quickly along the river's edge, jumping over downed logs and skirting large boulders. The closer he got, the surer he was. The illusive Albert stood fishing by the river. He stopped beside him taking great gulps of air. "I can't believe my eyes. Is it really you?"

"It's me, your twin," he smiled. He was wearing the same beige shirt and gray shorts he had been wearing at their first encounter, also.

"I, I, thought I would never see you again," Jule stammered. "I was beginning to think I just imagined you."

"Well, as you can see, I'm not a figment of your imagination. I'm very real. Another bad day at school, eh. Luckily, summer vacation begins soon."

Jule was curious to know how he knew he was having a bad day and that summer vacation was only a couple of days away. "Tyler, the jerk, was trying to pick a fight."

"Tyler the jerk. Is that his last name?"

"No silly. He's just a jerk that really needs to be taught a lesson." There was a confused look on Albert's face. It was the same look he gave if he didn't understand something. "I guess I should explain what a jerk is."

"Please do."

"A jerk is an annoyingly stupid or foolish person. That definitely sums up Tyler."

"I see." Albert tried to think of someone who fit this description, but couldn't.

"He's also a bully. He continually wants to start a fight with me. And once again today, Tyler was really asking for it."

Now Albert was really confused. "Asking for it?"

"He was making fun of me again and wanted me to fight with him."

"What's a fight?"

Jule looked up into the sky then turned to face Albert. "You don't know what a fight is?"

"Can't say I do."

He thought everyone knew about fighting. "It's when you hit somebody and they hit you back."

"I see. Why would you do that?"

Jule turned his gaze back to the heavens and gave the question some thought before he answered. "Hopefully, it will stop them from bothering you."

"I see," though he really didn't. "Where do you hit them?"

"Wherever you can. Usually in the face or stomach. Gee Albert. Haven't you ever gotten into a fight?"

"No."

"Have you ever seen anyone fight?"

Where he came from, there was never any need to fight. "No."

Man, he must be from another world, Jule concluded.

"Would you like to fish?" Albert asked, changing the subject.

"Sure," he said, taking the rod from Albert. Jule stood silently examining it from top to bottom.

"It's the Shakespear Ugly Stik that I gave you for your birthday. Is there a problem with it?"

Just when he thought he had solved the mystery around the Ugly Stik, Albert hands it to him. "There's a big problem with it," Jule began. "Some really strange things have happened since that time we first met," he began, handing the rod back to him and starting to walk back to where he left his backpack. "I'll start with the fishing rod. My parents gave me a Shakespeare Ugly Stik for my birthday."

"Isn't that what you wanted?" Albert said, following close behind him.

"Yes it is. But I concluded that my parents found the one you left in the oak tree out back and wrapped it up for my birthday. And Kristen gave me a No. 10 Hare's Ear Nymph, which is identical to the one you gave me. I have spent hours trying to figure this out ..."

"Figure what out?"

"Kristen! What are you doing here? You scared the wits out of me!" he exclaimed, looking up from the ground. "How did you find me?"

"I heard you and Dad talking about this place when you came back from fishing on your birthday. I figured you would be here when I didn't see you at school."

Nosy Kristen strikes again. So much for my secret place, though there was still the spot with Albert down river she didn't know about. "But, how did you get here?" He knew she'd never run here like he did.

"Erin's mom drove her home to get the present she forgot for her teacher. I hitched a ride so I could save your butt. Now hurry up! Lunchtime is almost over and we have to get back to Erin's house or we won't get a drive back to school. Hopefully your teacher didn't call Mom," she added.

Jule picked up his backpack and quickly glanced behind him, and then skyward. Albert had disappeared but the osprey was back, circling aimlessly above.

"What are you looking at now?" she asked, worrying they wouldn't get to Erin's house.

"Nothing. Come on, let's go."

They ran as fast as they could to Erin's house. Kristen was surprised that she couldn't keep up with Jule. He had to slow down or stop for her many times. She vowed to do more running this summer. It was embarrassing to have her little brother outrun her.

During the ride back to school, Jule sat quietly eating his lunch in the backseat, thinking about his meeting with Albert. As they drove up in front of the school, the bell sounded. Kristen and Erin went in the front of the school and Jule ran for the side entrance. He was walking toward the back of the classroom when Ms. Annadale asked to see him in the hall. "I hope you have a good reason for not being in class after recess this morning," she sighed. He had been so good lately, that she had almost forgotten that he skipped school periodically.

He didn't have a reason. Well, not one he was going to tell her. He knew he was in trouble, once again, for skipping. He had hoped that she wouldn't notice. Being the second last day of school, there were several empty desks in the classroom of lucky kids who started vacation early. He stood still, staring at the floor.

"When you didn't come in from recess, I figured you had skipped off school. Your sister confirmed it when she came to the classroom looking for you. She also informed me about the incident with Tyler. Kristen was quite sure she knew where you would be and volunteered to go and get you during lunch period. She asked me to hold off calling your mom. I explained to her that school policy stipulates I must always report a missing student to the office. Mrs. Campbell tried your house and the shop where your mother works and she wasn't at either place. When she sees the attendance sheet, she will know you have returned, so lucky for you, a call to your mom won't be necessary. But, that doesn't mean you are out of the woods for skipping school. Now, I have to get back into the classroom," she said, glancing at her watch. "We'll discuss this further at afternoon recess." Jule nodded then turned and walked behind her into the classroom. Ms. Annadale told the students they could read, write, do art work or chat quietly to each other.

Jule opened up his very worn novel entitled, *'Molly Moon's Incredible Book of Hypnotism'*, that he had read and reread many times. He became interested in the super natural at an early age. He opened the novel, pretending to read it. He thought about his encounter with the illusive Albert. One thing was sure. He is real. Jule believed there was a connection between Albert and the osprey. He also felt that Albert was connected in some way to every strange occurrence, including the honey bee, that happened lately.

When the recess bell sounded, Jule remained at his desk waiting for Ms. Annadale. He knew he should have stayed and ignored Tyler, but as it turned out, he was glad he had gone to his thinking place and met up with Albert. Ms.

Annadale called him to her desk and pointed to the chair beside it, then asked what happened at recess this morning.

Jule shifted a little in his chair before answering. He hated confrontations like this. "I had a slight misunderstanding with one of the older kids."

"I see. This slight misunderstanding must have been upsetting enough for you to leave school. Do you want to tell me about it?"

Jule looked up from his hands and faced Ms. Annadale. She was very pretty with her auburn hair tied back and sharp brown eyes. "One of the kids was trying to provoke a fight by shoving me to the ground, but another kid stepped in to help me. I don't need anyone to help me though," he added quickly. "So, rather than getting into a fight, I ran to my thinking place."

"Your thinking place?"

"Yes. Don't you have a thinking place, Ms. Annadale?"

"No, I can't say I do. Tell me about your thinking place."

"Well, mine is located deep in a forest, away from everyone. It's a place where I can be by myself, do some thinking, and connect with nature."

"It sounds like a wonderful place. Tell me, were you thinking of the consequences of running off to your thinking place?"

He wanted to tell her that it didn't matter, especially today, because he had a chance meeting with Albert. He nodded yes.

"Jule, when one of my favourite students goes missing, I become very worried."

"I didn't mean to worry you," he said sincerely. "It's just that I like to work things out for myself and do a better job of it at my thinking place."

Jule's Story

She admired his independence and found him to be much more mature than most kids his age. "I want you to promise me, if there is ever another incident where you feel you have to leave school, you will come straight to me or if I'm not here, another teacher. Then we can take the necessary steps to remedy the situation."

"I promise."

"You are a very special young man, Jule. I am very proud of you. I have enjoyed having you in my class this year."

"Thanks. You're my favourite teacher. So far," he added.

"Thank you," she smiled. "You can go outside now and join your friends. Oh, and keep up your writing. You really do have a wonderful imagination."

"I will," he said, as he walked out of the classroom.

The school bus pulled up in front of the house. Kristen disembarked first, with Jule close behind. "Only one more day," Kristen sighed, unlocking the backdoor after school.

"I wonder where Mom is?" Jule asked, opening the refrigerator.

"Probably shopping. You know how she always buys us something special for passing. By the way, did you get in trouble for skipping school?"

"Not really. Ms. Annadale and I talked about it at recess. She told me that they couldn't get a hold of Mom and because I came back, the secretary stopped trying."

"Lucky for you little brother. But that doesn't mean I won't let the cat out of the bag," she smiled confidently. She loved being one up on him.

"Go ahead and tell Mom," Jule said, before shoving a piece of banana bread in his mouth.

"Tell Mom what?" she asked, coming in the backdoor.

They both looked wide-eyed as Mom came into the kitchen loaded with eco bags. "How much we love you," Kristen smiled sweetly.

"Yeah," Jule added.

"Aw, isn't that sweet."

"Where were you? We were beginning to worry," Kristen said, trying to peek in the bags Mom had left by the door.

"You'll spoil your surprise, my dear," Mom said, sitting down hard on a kitchen chair.

"Well at least you are home now," Jule said, hugging her around the neck. "Can I go fishing until supper?"

The hug surprised her. Ever since he started getting himself up, she had missed their morning routine. "Yes dear. Supper's at six."

She turned and looked at Kristen. "You can help me put away the groceries dear daughter and tell me about your day."

Jule grabbed his Shakespeare Ugly Stik by the door, ran as fast as he could to the river, and stood where he and Albert had met this morning. He decided to try calling his name, then waited patiently for him to appear. When it became apparent that Albert would be a no-show, he looked up at the place in the sky where the osprey circled and sure enough, it was riding peacefully on the air currents. Though he was quite sure there was a connection with Albert and the osprey, he wasn't sure what it was. It seemed when one was around, the other wasn't. It was one of the many mysteries he wanted to discuss with Albert, whenever they met again. He was content with the fact that Albert was real. But how real, he wondered as he cast his line. Kristen hadn't said anything this morning when she came here to get him and Albert had been right behind him. *One thing's for sure, if she had seen him, she would have said something.* He thought about all the questions he wanted to ask Albert. The most important question was where he was from. He was almost convinced, with all the research he'd done lately about the universe that it was quite possible Albert was from another world. Also, he may possess some magical powers. He seemed to appear and disappear. The sound of distant thunder interrupted his thoughts. The sunny sky was filling up with large white fluffy thunder heads. He noticed that the osprey wasn't circling above, as he quickly reeled in his line and began walking back through the woods. As the intensity of the lightning and thunder picked up, he ran the rest of the way home arriving at the back door just as the sky opened up. He remembered all too well what getting drenched with rain felt like.

"Good timing," Dad said, greeting him at the door.

"I know the rule Dad. At the first sign of an approaching storm, I'm to come straight home," Jule said as thunder sounded.

"That's my boy." He could tell by the good mood his dad was in that Kristen hadn't spilled the beans about him skipping out at recess. "It must be a nice feeling knowing you only have one more day of school before summer vacation begins."

"It sure is," Jule smiled. He could hardly wait.

9

ON THE LAST day of school, students spent the time cleaning out their desks and helping the teacher put the classroom in order for September. At lunchtime, Ms. Annadale ordered in pizza from Ray's Pizza in the village, as a treat for the kids. It was a great ending to a good school year for all her students. They said their goodbyes then headed outside to wait for the school buses to arrive. Dismissal was an hour earlier and for Jule, that translated into more time to fish. With a little luck, Albert would be waiting for him down by the river. He stood chatting with some kids as they waited by the curb for the bus, when someone pointed up toward a bird floating aimlessly on the wind currents in the sky just above them. They were all staring up trying to figure out what kind of bird it was.

"It's an osprey," Jule said, wondering why it was circling above the school.

Tyler and some of his friends just happened to be walking by. Jule knew it was not a coincidence. Tyler's bus loading area was at the back of the school. He asked what everyone was looking up at, and one of the students told him about the osprey.

"It's not an osprey. It's a turkey vulture," he said, watching it fly in circles. "Everyone knows that vultures circle in the sky like that when they're looking for dead meat," he said, glancing toward Jule.

Jule looked Tyler in the eye. "It's an osprey," he contradicted, purposely trying to bug Tyler. After all, it was the last day of school and all the kids were standing around so there wouldn't be much he could do to him.

"Well, if it isn't Mr. Knowitall himself," Tyler said, walking toward him, as the kids stepped back clearing a path for him. He had been hoping to get at Jule once more before school ended and here was his chance. He stopped a couple of centimeters in front of him. "Now, what kind of bird is it?" he asked, in a threatening tone.

Jule raised his right hand in protest. Suddenly, Tyler fell back hard on his butt. It happened so quickly and swiftly, he didn't have time to stop himself from falling. He looked up at Jule and was just about to say something, but his butt hurt so badly, for once he was speechless.

The stunned look on Jule's face said it all. *What happened? I never even touched him.* The kids began laughing as Tyler tried to stand up, but couldn't.

"Look," one of the kids said, pointing to a large nearby maple tree. "It's an osprey!"

As everyone turned to look, the bird took off flying higher and higher in the sky until it disappeared over the school, just as the buses began arriving. The driver for Jule's bus opened the door and asked if Tyler was okay. "He pushed me," he said, pointing at Jule from his spot on the ground. He was still quite shaken and upset.

"I didn't touch him," Jule said, still trying to figure out what happened.

Jule's Story

"Come on son. Get up now and run for your bus. It's summer vacation," the driver smiled.

The kids began boarding the bus. Jule took his usual seat at the back. It was a perfect vantage point to see Tyler still sitting on the grass beside the sidewalk. He watched as Tyler's friends literally had to pull him up onto his feet. He stood up, rubbing his tender backside and spotted Jule staring out a window near the back of the bus. "I'll get you, you little jerk," he yelled, flipping the bird as an afterthought. Jule just smiled and waved as the doors shut, and the bus pulled away from the curb. He sat back in his seat reliving the non-contact shove he gave Tyler concluding he got what was coming to him. Thinking about the incident he was sure he had witnessed something similar, and just before the bus pulled up in front of his house, he remembered. The only time he had ever seen anything fall so hard on its butt was when Albert put up his hand to stop the charging bear the first day they had met.

When the bus door opened, Jule was first off and ran straight for the back door. He handed his report card to Mom then grabbed his fishing rod. He had passed, with honours, into grade five. "I'll be home for supper," he said, running out the door with his old fishing rod to the river. He looked up at the clear blue sky for the osprey and couldn't see it. He drew in a breath of warm air, then sat on a log at the river's edge and cast his line. It felt so good to be on vacation. *Nothing but fishing and more fishing. No school for two whole months!*

"Well, I see you are enjoying our favourite past time."

"Albert! You scared the wits out of me. Although I should be used to you popping in and out of my life." He was glad to see him as he quickly reeled in his line. "Now that you are here, I think it's time we have a good long talk. That is if you have the time."

"I have lots of time now. Let's go back to where we first met," Albert said, leading the way. *He definitely knows his way around* Jule noted as they walked back to his thinking place in the woods. Side by side, they sat on a downed ash tree. "You look exactly like me," Jule said shaking his head, as he stared at Albert. "It's like looking at myself in a mirror."

"A mirror?"

"Don't tell me you don't know what a mirror is?"

"Then I won't. But I don't."

Jule stared wide-eyed at Albert trying to figure out how to describe one. "It's this piece of glass with something coated on the back of it so you can't see through it. And when you look in it, you can see yourself."

"Why do you want to see yourself?"

He was puzzled by Albert's question. *Everyone uses a mirror.* "So you can see if your face is clean or your hair is combed. Girls use a mirror the most. My sister is always in front of one," Jule said, blinking his eyes rapidly.

"Is there something wrong with your eyes?"

"No," he laughed. "I was just mimicking Kristen."

Jule turned to face Albert. "I have so many questions to ask you, I don't even know where to begin?"

"Well, it is always best to start at the beginning."

Jule thought back to their very first meeting. He had skipped school to come to his thinking place and Albert appeared out of nowhere. "Where did you come from?"

"I come from a place just beyond your imagination."

"You told me that the first day we met. That night, I was lying on my bed studying my galaxy posters on the ceiling and wondered if you are from another universe." Jule felt his heart race as he turned to face Albert. "Are you from another universe?" he asked, swallowing hard.

"Yes. I come from a planet just beyond Pluto."

"Sedna!"

"Yes. Do you know about my planet?"

Jule jumped up from the log. "I don't believe this! I read about Sedna in my astronomy magazine just recently."

"What did you read?" Albert asked curiously.

"Well, first off, some astronomers are saying that if Pluto is a planet, Sedna is clearly a planet too. Secondly, some scientists say there is no use calling Sedna a planet, because like Pluto, it's probably uninhabited. But that's not true." He turned slowly to face Albert. His mind was racing as he sat down quickly beside Albert feeling like he'd just discovered the biggest secret in the world. "How did you get here? What is it like? Do you have family? Have you got any friends?"

"Slow down Jule," Albert said, getting up from the log. "It is impossible for me to answer all your questions at once."

Jule apologized and sat tight-lipped as Albert began to talk. "To set the record straight, Sedna is a planet. Do you remember the story you read to your class?"

"Peaceful Pluto?" Jule said, wondering how Albert knew this.

"I come from a place, just beyond your imagination."

"You said that the day we met. Now I get it. Sedna is just beyond Pluto."

"That's correct. And strangely enough, your description of peaceful Pluto is almost a duplicate of Sedna," Albert smiled.

Jule jumped up from the log. "Wow! This is unbelievable. I had hoped there was a place like that somewhere in the universe." His studies about the vastness of our universe and those beyond definitely supported the theory that there could be life elsewhere. But, he had no idea that life existed in the universe that earth was a part of, though he had always hoped there was. "This is amazing! I wish I could visit Sedna one day," Jule smiled, gazing up at the vast blue sky. He turned toward Albert then joined him again on the log. There was still the matter of the fishing rods. "Did you leave the Shakespeare Ugly Stik you gave me, the day we first met, in the oak tree out back so that my parents could re-gift it for my birthday?" Jule was sure that he had and all he needed was Albert to confirm it once and for all.

"You mean this rod?" he smiled, reaching behind the log and handing it to him.

"How did you get that?" Jule asked, examining it from top to bottom.

"I brought it with me from Sedna."

"I'm confused. I have the identical rod my parents gave me for my birthday leaning against the wall in my bedroom. He looked at Albert. "So that means my parents didn't find the rod you left in the tree and re-gift it. They actually bought me a brand new Shakespeare Ugly Stik and No. 10 Ears Nymph. All this time, I thought my dad had found the rod you had left in the tree. You can understand why I thought that," he said, re-examining the Ugly Stik, once again. "They are absolutely identical."

"Not quite," Albert said, standing up beside Jule. "May I?" he smiled, taking the rod. He took hold of the black hand grip and gave it a quick turn. As he pulled it off the graphite pole, it made a loud popping noise. "Observe. The bottom of the hand grip comes off revealing the mark of Sedna. Now, look inside the hand grip," he said, passing it to Jule.

Jule looked inside and gasped loudly. "It's the same fishhook or 'J' shape that you whittled the stick to mount the steelhead I caught, surrounded by the most amazing colours! There's fuscia, mauve, green, turquoise, orange, silver, royal

Jule's Story

blue, cadmium yellow, gold, lime-green, purple," he said, soon realizing he could go on forever and still not name all the colours. It was difficult to imagine how so many different colours he hadn't even seen before, could be massed together in such a tiny space. "The only thing that even comes close is a kaleidoscope. But this is a million times better!" Jule exclaimed, turning to face him.

"These are the colours of Sedna," Albert replied, replacing the hand grip.

Jule sat back down on the log. "So my parents did give me a Shakespeare Ugly Stik for my birthday. But what about the No. 10 Ears Nymph that Kristen gave me?"

Albert removed the fly and placed it in Jule's hand. "What do you see?"

"An olive-gold Ear Nymph, exactly like the one Kristen gave me."

"Now, hold it up toward the sun and look again."

Jule held up the hook and let the sun do its magic. "Wow! Look at the colours! Again, I see every colour imaginable! This is awesome!"

"Once again, these are the brilliant colours of Sedna."

"But, did you leave this rod in the oak tree out back?" Jule asked, handing the hook back to Albert.

"Yes."

"Thank goodness. I thought I was seeing things when I saw it in the oak tree out back that was completely illuminated by this blinding." He stopped and turned to face Albert who seemed to be reading his mind. "Wait a minute. Was that your ...?"

"Beam of light," Albert smiled and nodded.

"Wow! How did you know what I was going to say?"

Though Albert always knew what Jule was thinking, he told him it is because they are twins.

Arlene Johnston

It was one thing to be one's twin and another to be a mind reader. "Albert you may be my twin, but I can't read other people's minds or make a bright beam shine down from the heavens." Still, Albert was identical. Jule had never imagined there could be anyone like himself. At times, he thought he was a little odd because he was more introverted than most kids his age. He would much rather be by himself fishing, hiking or just sitting quietly in the woods enjoying nature's gifts. Whether it was hand feeding chickadees or watching a moose and her calf wade into the river for food, he enjoyed this much more than computer games or watching television. And now he had a magical twin with the same interests.

"So Albert, did you take the rod from the tree?"

"Yes. I didn't want you to have to collect it during a thunderstorm, so I took it back to Sedna that night. If your mom hadn't caught sight of the racoon being chased by the cat, you would have had time to retrieve it before the storm."

Jule thought back to the storm. He had never been so frightened of one in his life. Usually, he enjoyed a thunderstorm and would sit in his room and watch until it passed. One particular time he had actually witnessed a lighting ball. He sat hypnotized and watched as a perfect circle of fire formed. As quickly as it began, it dissolved. So intense was the lightning ball that its image had imprinted itself on the back of his eyes. Minutes after experiencing this phenomenon, he could close his eyes and see it form and burn itself out many times, until it finally disappeared forever. "That was not a good storm to be out in. I had no sooner stood on the back of the bench when this blinding flash of lightning, followed by a humongous thunder, scared the wits out of me. At that point, all I wanted to do was get back into my room. And to make matters worse, once I finally got back onto the roof in the pouring rain, I tried to open the window and it wouldn't budge. I thought for sure someone must have locked it. But then when I tried again, after the storm passed, it opened." Jule turned and looked at Albert. "Why do I have this feeling that you know all about this?"

"Because, if I hadn't unlocked the window, you would have spent the night on the roof."

"It was locked? You were in my room? How in the world did you do that?"

"Let's just say I have my ways."

Jule looked at his watch. "I had better get going. I'm not even sure I thanked my family for my birthday gifts. I was so sure that they had found the Shakespeare Ugly Stik in the oak tree and re-gifted it. Now I know for sure that they really did buy me a new rod and No. 10 Ear Nymph." Jule felt better than he had in a long time. Finally, the Shakespeare Ugly Stik mystery had been solved.

Mom waited patiently for Dad to come home from work and as he walked in the back door, she began. "Hon, I think I have the answer why Jule has been acting so strange lately. He has a girlfriend! I found his little friend's phone number in his shirt pocket when I emptied it before I did the laundry."

Somehow, Dad wasn't as convinced. "Just because you find some girl's number in his pocket."

"There's a beautifully coloured red heart by her name," she added, pointing to it on the paper.

"I guess that'll do it," he smiled.

"Did I hear you say Jule has a girlfriend?" Kristen asked, walking into the kitchen. "Her name wouldn't happen to be Natalie would it?"

"Do you know her?" Dad asked, reaching into the refrigerator for a bottle of water.

"Oh yeah. Everyone on our school bus knows about her crush on him. 'Don't forget to call me, Jule'," she mimicked.

"Now Kristen, don't be catty."

"Well, he brings up Adam Fullerton any chance he gets."

"I know sweetheart, but you know how your brother likes to keep to himself. Speaking of which, he should be heading home now."

"I'll go find him," Kristen said, running out the backdoor.

"Something's up," Dad remarked, as she slammed the porch door.

Kristen grabbed her olive green coloured mountain bike and started riding down the road as Jule and Albert were just about to round the last bend. "So Albert, why is it when anyone comes on the scene you disappear? Maybe if you stuck around more, it wouldn't be so difficult explaining your existence," Jule said, kicking at a stone on the road. He was so busy concentrating on kicking one particular pink and grey stone, that he didn't see Kristen.

"You do like to talk to yourself little brother."

"Kristen! You gotta stop startling me like that, you jerk!"

"Oh Jule. If you kept your head up, you would have seen me. I'm only here to deliver you a message. Mom and Dad know all about Natalie," she said smugly.

"What about her?"

"Just that she gave you her phone number and you were stupid enough to leave it in your shirt pocket. Mom found it before she washed it."

"So."

"So! It had a great big red heart on it! Natalie loves Jule. Natalie loves Jule."

"Can it Kristen!"

"No way! Natalie loves Jule! Natalie loves Jule! You better get your butt home for supper!" she yelled, before quickly riding off. He hadn't even bothered looking at Natalie's note. In fact, he had totally forgotten about it. *Great!* He had just given Kristen all the ammunition she needed to bug him for the rest of summer vacation.

"That must be Kristen."

"Albert! Where did you go?"

"Into thin air. I figured you had enough to deal with when I saw her coming."

Jule looked toward the bend in the road. "How did you see her?"

"Can't get into it now. Your dad will be rounding the bend shortly. Next time we meet, bring a mirror."

Jule stood and watched, as his father came into view. *Albert, you are amazing!*

"Hi Son," Dad called out and waved.

"Hey Dad," he waved back, looking over his shoulder before running toward him. True to his word, Albert just disappeared into thin air.

"Any fish?"

"Not today. But there's always tomorrow," Jule smiled. He hadn't caught any fish since that first time with Albert.

"Dad, I really love my Shakespeare Ugly Stik that you and Mom gave me for my birthday."

"I'm glad son. It was the one you kept hinting at."

"I really appreciate it. Thanks." They chatted back and forth for the remainder of the walk home.

"No luck fishing?" Mom asked, as she prepared supper.

"Not today. Thanks again for my fishing rod, Mom. I really do like it. Jule stood his old rod near the back door then headed upstairs to wash up and think about Albert. He still had a ton of questions to ask him. Starting with how he knew about the cat chasing the racoon the night of the storm. And the osprey floating on wind currents in the sky down by the river, but only if Albert doesn't appear. Then there's his disappearing act. *That would be neat*, Jule thought wishing he could do that. He could hardly wait to meet with Albert again. He picked up the Shakespeare Ugly Stik that was standing beside his bed and tried to pull off the handgrip. It wouldn't budge. Final proof that his parents had truly bought it for his birthday.

After supper, Jule excused himself and went to his room. He laid down on his bed to look at his galaxy posters, focusing his eyes on Pluto, and then just beyond. "There it is!" He stood up on his bed to get a closer look. "There's Sedna, where Albert is from!"

"Albert?" Kristen said, walking by his partially open door.

He knew she would never believe him, but he told her anyway. "My twin."

"Here we go again! Why don't you save your imagination for writing your dumb stories?" Inside, she was very jealous of her brother's creativity. "I was going to ask if you wanted to bike into town for an ice cream cone."

Jule loved *Kawartha Dairy* ice cream, especially in the summer when there were so many more flavours to choose from. "Are you paying?"

"Maybe." She wasn't going to mention that Dad had given her the money.

"In that case, let's go!" he said, jumping off the bed.

They collected their bikes and helmets from the shelter at the side of the house then rode the bike paths into downtown Haliburton. With summer vacation in full swing, it was much busier now. They managed to score a picnic table in Head Lake Park close to where the river widened into the lake, and then took turns going to the ice cream parlour.

Jule's Story

Not long ago, the newly renovated barn that used to house Rachael's bakery, had been converted into an old fashioned ice cream parlour. Patrons could sit at round, frosted, plexiglass tables covered with cadmium yellow and cobalt blue checkered tablecloths. Each table had three white wrought iron chairs with seat cushions that matched the table coverings. Five snow white ceiling fans circulated the sweet smell of ice cream, candy and baked goods throughout the parlour. A choice of more than 50 flavours of premium *Kawartha Dairy* ice cream kept the parlour hopping with a constant flow of customers. If ice cream wasn't your choice, wooden shelves mounted on the walls were full of clear glass candy jars filled with individually wrapped multicoloured sticks of candy and gum. Open boxes of chocolates made by a local artisan in every imaginable flavour sat beckoning in two large temperate glass counters. Patrons could choose from a wide variety of chocolates. Once again, the selection was endless. You could purchase them one at a time, or make a selection of any amount that could be gift wrapped in your choice of multicoloured papers. And if that wasn't enough, a selection of homemade pies, tarts, cookies, multi-grained breads and preserves were waiting in a long glass counter close to the exit.

As usual, the joint was jumping. Jule didn't mind the wait, as he savoured the sights and smells, in one of three long line-ups. He especially loved the colourful atmosphere with every colour imaginable popping up somewhere in the parlour. He watched as the tourists looked around in awe, especially the children that came in. Squeals of joy and excitement filled the parlour as Jule ordered a three-scoop moose tracks waffle cone, and then reluctantly went back so Kristen could get hers. He told her about the crowds and the long line-ups, but she didn't mind either. Everyone knows the ice cream parlour is the best place in town.

"What kind did you get?" he asked, when she returned. His was long gone by the time she got back to the table.

"Blueberry cheesecake, with rainbow sprinkles."

Jule looked toward Kristen, as she finished off the last of her cone. "By the way, thanks for the No. 10 Ear Nymph."

"You're welcome. What made you think of that?" she asked, wiping her face with a royal blue and yellow striped serviette.

"I just wanted you to know I really appreciate the gift, that's all."

"Did you know that Mom and Dad thought you didn't like the fishing rod they got you?"

It was no wonder. He had shown no excitement at all. In fact, it was a totally opposite reaction to what they had expected. If it hadn't been for Albert beating them to the punch, he would have been so excited. "I really do appreciate the Shakespeare Ugly Stik they gave me. I told them so today."

"We all went out together to get your gifts."

"Really?" he smiled, wiping his face with his hankie, wishing he had known that on his birthday. He had been so confused. Up until today, he still believed his parents had somehow gotten hold of Albert's Ugly Stik and re-gifted it. Though he was satisfied with Albert's explanation regarding the difference between the two rods, Jule's gut feeling was that there may be more to this, but he couldn't quite put his finger on it. It all seemed so strange that his identical twin, from Sedna, appeared at his thinking place and just happened to give him the Shakespeare Ugly Stik he had always wanted for his upcoming birthday.

Jule's Story

"You were off fishing the day we went," Kristen continued, breaking his train of thought. "We got it from that sports shop right over there. You gave us enough hints," she added.

Jule chuckled when he thought of all the advertisements from his fishing magazine he had left around the house. He hounded his parents until a week before his birthday. "Thanks for telling me this." He felt better knowing all the facts. Still, something didn't seem right and he vowed to spend his free time this summer figuring it out.

They sat quietly and watched some older kids swinging back and forth on an old tire that had been tied with thick rope to a large willow tree branch jutting out over the river. As they swung over the deepest part of the river, they would let go and swim to shore. Timing was very important, as there was only one deep pocket surrounded by rocky, shallow water.

"That looks like fun," Jule said.

"Don't even think about it! One wrong move and the paramedics would be transporting your stupid butt to emergency."

"Oh Kristen, where's your sense of adventure?" They were quite different that way. Jule was into nature and adventure, while Kristen was into to her friends and her bedroom mirror. She would spend hours trying on different outfits with hair styles she had seen in *Teen Vogue* and now that she was going into grade eight, Mom had agreed to go with her to *Rexall* to purchase lipstick, eye shadow and blush. She could hardly wait.

"We'd better get going. It's starting to get dark and Dad wants to have a bonfire," Kristen said, putting her serviette in the trash can.

It was a beautiful summer evening, perfect for a bonfire. By the time they reached home, Dad had the fire crackling and sparking. They stood and watched him add more twigs, and old wood pieces he had been saving to burn. Kristen and Jule fetched some plastic chairs from under the top deck and began placing them around the pit. The whole family enjoyed sitting around the fire talking and telling stories. Mom always had lots of goodies to roast over the fire. Once it settled down a bit she began opening packages of marshmallows and wieners while the kids searched for four strong sticks.

Eventually, everyone sat down around the fire, and began spearing marshmallows and wieners onto the end of their sticks. "Hey Dad, do you want to go fishing tomorrow morning?" Jule asked, stabbing four marshmallows and two wieners on the end his stick.

"Sounds good to me, Son." He had not lived up to his word of doing more fishing. But, tomorrow morning was the beginning of two weeks of vacation and he planned on fishing with Jule at every chance.

They sat quietly roasting their goodies over the fire when suddenly a long, brilliant, white light streaked quickly through the sky turning the dark night into day. "Oh my goodness! What's that?" Kristen cried, pointing toward the object.

"Wow! It looks like a meteorite!" Dad said, gazing skyward. "You don't get to see one of those too often."

"Maybe we should make a wish," Mom said, watching it cross the sky.

"It's Albert!" Jule yelled, confidently knowing he's the only one who could light up the sky like that.

"Albert?" Mom said, as the sky turned black again.

"My twin."

Jule's Story

"Are you on that stupid kick again?"

"It's not a stupid kick, Kristen. Albert really is my twin and he's from Sedna."

They all thought his story about Albert was just that, a story. He had tried to convince them numerous times that Albert was real, but with no luck. Now after witnessing Albert's powerful display, Jule thought this was his chance to really convince his family once and for all.

"Sedna?" Dad said. *There's a new one.*

"The planet Sedna is located just past Pluto and may soon be recognized as the tenth planet in our solar system," Jule said, removing a *Maple Leaf* wiener from the package and mounting it on the end of his stick. "Now that my twin, Albert from Sedna, has appeared, astronomers who are convinced there is no life beyond Pluto, will have no choice but to include Sedna as a recognizable planet in our solar system." It was strange to hear Jule talk about people living on another planet. He spoke as if they were living just down the road.

Kristen, as usual, had little patience with his story telling. Although, she had to admit, he was very good at it. "Now I've heard everything. Where do you come up with this stuff?"

Mom and Dad agreed he had a vivid imagination.

"This is not something I imagined." He thought for sure they would believe him, as he continued. "I was with Albert at my fishing spot just this afternoon. Dad, you remember where we fished on my birthday. That's where I met up with him again." Jule looked over at him for support. "Up until today, I thought I was imagining him. But I'm not. He's real."

"You are so weird," Kristen said.

"Really. Well when you rode up on your bike just before supper and asked me if I was talking to myself, I was talking to Albert."

"I didn't see any Albert."

This was always the most difficult part to explain. Whenever Jule needed him, Albert vanished "He tends to disappear when people come around."

"So, we're back to your imaginary friend," Dad smiled, placing a marshmallow on the end of his stick.

Jule stood his ground. "No Dad. Albert is real. He was with me when you came to meet me tonight. But again, he disappeared. Here's something else," he added. "They don't have mirrors on Sedna and next time we meet, he wants me to bring one. Even I don't have that good of an imagination to think that up," he said, hoping they would believe his story now.

"How do they know how they look?" Mom asked, reaching into the marshmallow bag.

She sounded like a typical woman. Here he was trying to tell her about his twin from Sedna and she wants to know how they look at themselves. "How should I know?" he said, throwing up his hand. "We never got that far. I had so many questions, I didn't get a chance to ask about mirrors."

"Well that certainly would be the first question I'd ask," Kristen said, throwing back her long blond hair and wishing there was one close by so she could see if she had any marshmallow on her face.

Jule pressed on. "Dad, do you remember the night you thought you saw me in the backyard during that thunderstorm?" He didn't wait for his answer. "Well, it was me." He looked over at his dad who seemed lost in thought. He could tell by all their faces that their memory needed refreshing, once again. "It was the same night I tried to

Jule's Story

explain how I caught the fish with the Shakespeare Ugly Stik Albert gave me for my birthday."

"I remember now. You got angry with your sister and I told you to excuse yourself from the dinner table."

"That's right. It was the day I skipped school and you came looking for me."

"The day we were so worried about you," Mom added.

"Yes. I invited Albert to dinner, but again he disappeared because somehow he knew Dad was on his way to meet me."

"Was that the night the ruffed grouse was running across the road?"

"Yes!"

"You should have seen that bird run. It looked so funny running across the road with its elongated neck leading the way." Dad chuckled.

Jule made a mental note to ask Albert if there was a connection between him and the grouse. He was almost positive that Albert could transform himself into anything he wanted. "Anyway," he continued, "at some point after that, he placed the Shakespeare Ugly Stik he'd given me for my birthday on the lowest branch of that oak tree," Jule said, pointing toward it. The firelight cast a bright orange glow on the huge tree as the flames danced in the evening sky, hypnotizing him for the moment. *If only the tree could have been lit like that ...*

"Jule. Is that the end of your story?" Dad asked, snapping him out of his trance.

"Where was I? Oh yeah. I discovered it when I got out of bed to look at this bright beam of light shining on the branch that led my eyes right to the rod."

"Oh, brother. Now I've heard everything," Kristen said, throwing her head back and looking skyward.

"Continue Jule," Dad encouraged.

"In the meantime, Mom came upstairs to say good night."

"I remember now. It was the night the cat chased the racoon over the shed," she chuckled. "You should have seen that poor racoon trying to escape the neighbour's cat."

"That stupid black and white striped cat from way down the road?" Kristen asked.

"Yeah, that's the one." They continued talking about the cat until Jule interrupted.

"After you left my room, Mom, I tried to see if my Ugly Stick was still in the oak tree, but it was too dark. Then a thunderstorm began approaching. There was a flash of lightning that lasted long enough for me to see it sitting on the branch where Albert had left it. I knew it was now or never to retrieve the rod. It was just after ten. You were both up and watching television in the great room, so going out the backdoor was definitely out. There was only one way out the back and that was to climb out of my bedroom window onto the roof ..."

"Wait a minute," Dad interrupted. "That was the night I thought I saw you running through the yard in the storm. But that couldn't be because I went up and checked on you, and you were in bed asleep."

Jule was glad his decoy had worked. He debated on telling him about it and decided not to, as he might need to use it again. Thankfully Mom spoke up. "You were on the roof? During a storm? You could have been struck by lightning."

"Mom, I used the lightning flashes to guide me to the tree. Otherwise, I would never have found my way."

"Carry on," Dad said impatiently.

"By the time I made it to the tree, pulled the wrought iron bench under the branch, and stood on the back of it, there was a wicked flash of lightning that scared the wits out

Jule's Story

of me. I lost my balance and fell to the ground. Then the sky opened up soaking me to the bone. Needless to say, the pouring rain vetoed my plan, so I couldn't retrieve the rod. When I checked to see if it was still in the tree the next day, it wasn't there. So, when my birthday came and I got a Shakespeare Ugly Stik, I thought for sure that Dad had located Albert's fishing rod and re-gifted it. That's why I wasn't excited on my birthday." Jule took a bite of a well-done marshmallow, and a mouthful of orange crush, before proceeding. "But today when I met Albert, he straightened out the riddle that has plagued me since my birthday."

"Which was?" Dad said.

"That the Shakespeare Ugly Stik you gave me, was not the one he gave me."

"I could have told you that," Dad said, stabbing a marshmallow.

"I realize that now," Jule sighed. "Before Albert solved the riddle for me today, I was very confused because the rods are identical, except for one thing. Removing the hand grip on the Ugly Stik Albert gave me, reveals the mark of Sedna, which is shaped like a fishhook or a 'J' surrounded by the most vibrant shades of greens, yellows, pinks, blues, reds, purples, oranges ... I could go on naming them forever. I have never seen such amazing colours in my whole life!" he said excitedly, jumping up from his chair. "The best way to describe it, is like looking into a kaleidoscope only a zillion times better! It's also the same shape as the stick he whittled to mount the fish on because I didn't have my stringer. Remember Dad. You said I did such a good job whittling the stick. I didn't do it. Albert did," he said as convincingly as he could. "And we all enjoyed the fish the next night for supper," he added sitting back down in his chair and watching as his family absorbed the information he had given them.

It was no surprise that Kristen was first to break the silence. "Mom, Dad, you don't really believe all this Albert, Sedna, vibrant colour stuff, do you?"

"He sure has your imagination, dear," Dad said, turning toward Mom.

"He's a much better storyteller than I could ever be."

His family continued talking and laughing back and forth, as if Jule was absent. *They don't believe me. They think it's a story I've made up.* He quickly realized that nothing he could say would make them believe him. He stood up and pitched his stick into the fire, and then began walking toward the house.

"Sweetheart. Where are you going?" Mom called out, as they watched him walk away. "We are just kidding around. We enjoy your stories."

"Especially the one about your twin from another planet," Kristen added, through her laughter.

"Honey, please come back," Mom continued coaxing, as she watched him open the backdoor. "Maybe we were a little too hard on him," she said, turning back to the fire.

"He'll be okay," Dad shrugged.

"Good night little bro," Kristen yelled, and was not surprised that he didn't answer.

Jule washed up, and then lay in bed shining his flashlight on Sedna. *I know Albert is my twin from Sedna.* He continued studying the small planet on the ceiling above him. He had told his family the truth about Albert and they still didn't believe him. *They think it's just one more imagined story.* He switched off his flashlight and turned onto his left side. *One day they will see.*

He fell asleep remembering what his father had said just a few weeks ago, 'the truth always comes out in the end'.

10

JULE GOT UP just before dawn. He found a small mirror under his bathroom sink that he put in his shirt pocket, just in case he met up with Albert. The house was quiet as he tiptoed down to the kitchen. He packed some blueberry-apple muffins, a banana, two apples, some almonds, and a bottle of apple juice into his backpack. Then he scooped a handful of sunflower seeds into a small plastic bag. "Breakfast on the go for everyone" he whispered, tucking the bag of seeds into the front pouch. He picked up his Shakespeare Ugly Stik and quietly closed the backdoor, then ran down the road and through the welcoming cool forest to his thinking place. The sun was just beginning to rise, as he sat down on a fallen ash tree to catch his breath.

Although it was already hot, the surrounding trees kept this area a few degrees cooler. He took an apple and muffin out of his backpack, and then sat and waited for the forest to come alive as the first rays of sunshine began filtering through the trees. *It is going to be a beautiful day* he thought taking a bite of his blueberry-apple muffin. *Mom makes the best muffins in the world* he decided.

Just as he began eating his apple, the chickadees appeared for their morning feed. He offered a handful of sunflower seeds with his free hand. There was something different about the way they were retrieving the seeds. The chickadees would take turns flying down quickly to scoop the seeds with much less chirping, and definitely no acrobatics. In fact, most chirps were warnings. They were definitely being more cautious. He watched one particular bird quickly scoop a seed and fly off to a nearby tree where five baby chickadees fluttered their wings and chirped, hoping to get the contents of the seed their mother held between her feet finally pecking it open. She would feed one of the babies, and then fly back to Jule's open hand to start the process all over again. The different chirps taught the young valuable lessons, teaching them to be cautious and vigilant throughout their lives. He had witnessed this at home with Claire who seldom came for her morning feedings. When she did visit, she would quickly scoop a seed from his hand then fly off to her nest to feed her offspring. Like the chickadees here in the woods, she was much more cautious now that she was a mother. He wanted to get some fishing done before the sun got too high. He placed the bag of seeds on top of his backpack knowing he would be returning later for a snack in the slightly cooler woods.

He made a bandana with his hankie, picked up his Ugly Stik, and then walked toward the river, hoping to have better luck today pulling in a fish. He hadn't caught a fish since that first meeting with Albert. Jule stood by the river's edge and cast off. He looked toward the sky where the osprey usually rode the wind currents and concluded it must be too early. He turned and looked down river.

"Morning Jule!"

Oh my goodness! He stood his Ugly Stik up against a poplar tree and quickly ran down to where Albert stood by the river. Breathless, he asked "what are you doing here?"

Jule's Story

"Fishing, of course. I am your twin. I've been here since just before dawn," he said, reeling in his line and turning to face Jule. "You had quite a time trying to convince your family about your twin from Sedna last night, eh?" Albert knew they were going to know the truth very soon.

Jule stared at his mirror image who just happened to have on the same dark-blue denim shorts, burgundy shirt, and sported an identical bandana on his head. "How did you know that, Albert?"

"I have my ways. Here," he said, handing Jule the Shakespeare Ugly Stik he had given him for his birthday. "First I want some answers," Jule said, handing back the rod. "Did you have anything to do with that bright light that streaked across the sky last night?"

Albert turned to face Jule. "How do you think I got back to Earth? That bright light is the tail from my space ship."

"What! You have a space ship?"

"You look surprised. It's the only transportation I have to get from Sedna to Earth."

Jule swallowed hard. He hadn't given any thought as to how Albert got back and forth. He was still having a hard time believing he had a twin from another planet. One thing's for sure, Albert was not from Earth. "Is there any connection between you and the osprey that just happens to appear when you aren't around and I'm fishing down river?"

"Look at that lower tree branch across the river," Albert said, pointing downstream.

Jule turned to his left and scanned the tree. On the middle branch of a large yellow birch, in clear view, sat an osprey staring back at him.

"How did you know it was there," he said, turning back to Albert. "Albert?" Jule turned back to the osprey that had also disappeared. "Ahhh!" he cried, as he felt a tap on his right shoulder. "Albert! What are you doing?" He stood staring wide-eyed at him. "You are the osprey!"

Albert nodded.

"That was you then? You transformed into the osprey that flew by me that day with the four-pound steelback in your talons. And you looked me right in the eye!" he added.

"It would have been rude to fly by and not acknowledge you somehow," Albert smiled.

"Was that the four-pounder I caught with the Shakespeare Ugly Stik you gave me that first day we met?"

"No Jule. It was just an example of what you could catch. There are lots of good sized trout in the river. You just have to be there at the right time and the right place. Besides, an osprey has to eat too."

"You ate the fish?"

"It's the mainstay of an osprey's survival," Albert chuckled, thinking nothing of it.

Jule's mind was racing. He thought back to the last time he had seen the osprey and it had been at school when one of the kids pointed to it sitting in a tree. It was the day that Jule had put up his hand and the gesture sent Tyler reeling back on his butt. Knowing that Albert was probably reading his mind, he turned to him and said, "The Tyler no contact shove."

"I figured you needed a helping hand, pardon the pun, so for a split second you became me."

"What! That can't be. I didn't feel anything different," Jule said, thinking back to the episode.

"That's the beauty of having a twin from Sedna. I can be anything I want to be. Including you. Besides, Tyler, like the bear, needed to be dealt with in a more aggressive way. The bee on his forehead as a warning didn't deter him. So I stung him when he began swiping at it. As you folks on Earth would say, `to try and take the sting out of him'. And even though Tyler kept up a good front, I really let him have it, as his behaviour was very unacceptable."

"That means that you were the honey bee on my Peaceful Pluto story!" He remembered how it moved with each word he read. "Were you in my bedroom the night I tried to show Kristen?"

"Yes. I had to introduce myself somehow. And seeing you are so connected to nature, what better way," Albert smiled.

Jule was stunned by Albert's admissions, but at least he knew he wasn't going bonkers. Lately with all these strange events happening in his life, he began to wonder. For whatever reasons, he had held onto the notion that Albert was connected in some way and today it had been verified. Albert was now his identical 'magical' twin from Sedna with the power to do anything he wants. Jule found it frightening, but at the same time exhilarating. "Wait a minute. I thought you didn't know what a fight is."

"If you think about my methods of dealing with those that are aggressive, there was no fight involved. In the case of the bear, all I did was raise my left hand. In Tyler's case, he swiped at the bee to try and knock it off his forehead, and a bee's natural defence is its stinger. And if you remember back to your last confrontation with Tyler, all you did was raise your right hand. So you see, there was no fighting involved. Until you explained what a fight was, I had no idea. Sedna is a peaceful planet with absolutely no violence. Kindness rules."

Knowing Jule had enough answers for now, Albert handed him the Shakespeare Ugly Stik he had given him for his birthday. "It's time to catch a fish."

Jule took the rod from Albert. He remembered the mirror in his pocket that he brought to show him, but decided it could wait. Albert was right. It was time to do some fishing and process all this new information. He cast off and as soon as the rig hit the water, a steelhead began thrashing on the end of the line. "Wow! It must be a four-pounder. This hasn't happened since the first time I fished with this rod."

"Sedna rods are far superior," Albert said proudly, as he stood by the shoreline watching Jule struggle to bring the fish in. "How about doing a catch and release today?"

"Are you crazy! This is for supper tonight," Jule said emphatically, as he brought the flipping specimen to his empty hand.

"How would you like to have supper on Sedna?"

"What?"

"You had said just the other day that you would like to visit my planet. Well, now's your chance."

Jule unhooked the fish then turned to face Albert. "I don't know about that."

"I doubt your family will miss you. Besides, we could be there and back before they do."

"Really?" *Then I could absolutely tell them about Sedna, not that they would probably believe me.* He was still very hurt about what transpired around the bonfire last night. *So much for telling the truth.*

Albert saw the disheartened look on Jule's face and asked him again. "Are you going to release the fish?"

Back home, the kitchen was sunny and bright, as Mom sat at the table with her morning coffee reading the *Globe and Mail*. She looked up from the paper as the kitchen door swung open.

"Morning hon," Dad said, entering the kitchen. "Is Jule up yet?"

"No. His door was shut, so I assume he's sleeping in," she replied, turning the page.

Jule's Story

"Didn't he say something about him and I going fishing today?"

"Yup. That was before we started making fun of his story. I feel really bad about that," she said, closing the paper. "I don't ever want him to stop using his imagination. He is an excellent storyteller."

"I think maybe we were all a little too hard on him. I'm going to see if he still wants to go," Dad said, putting down his coffee cup and heading upstairs. He knocked on the bedroom door. "Jule. Are you awake?" There was no answer. He quietly turned the door handle and peered into his room.

"Is he getting up?" Mom asked, when Dad quickly returned to the kitchen.

"It seems he's already up. His bed was left unmade and I found this article about Sedna lying on his pillow," Dad said, skimming through it. "Wait a minute. It looks like there really is a place called Sedna." Jule had quoted the article almost word for word last night. He rubbed his forehead trying to remember what else he said, handing the magazine to Mom.

"Oh my goodness! But it says here, they aren't sure if it's a planet." She thought back to last night and concluded that Jule might be using Sedna as a setting for a story he was writing. Still, she wasn't so sure this was a work of fiction. "What if he does have a twin?" she asked rereading the article.

"Are you two on about that again?" Kristen asked, sauntering into the kitchen.

"Read it for yourself," Mom said angrily, handing her the astronomy magazine. She wasn't sure who she was angry with, herself, Dad, Kristen or Jule. "In the meantime, where's Jule?" Her gut feeling said, `something's not right'.

"How should I know? I just got up," Kristen said yawning, as she began reading. "Knowing Jule, he's probably fishing," she said, closing the magazine. "I don't believe all that outer space crap anyway."

Mom ignored her comment and walked over to the back door. "His fishing rod is gone and so is his backpack. I have a strange feeling about all this," she said, starting to feel panicky. "Hon, we have to go find him."

Dad put down his coffee cup, as he tried to recall where they went fishing. "I'm not sure if I know how to get to where we fished by the river."

"I know where it is," Kristen said. "Thank goodness one of us listens in this family," she said, leading the way.

They quickly walked down the road in the hot sunshine trying to figure out the path Jule usually takes to the river. Dad stopped at the first one and was sure this was the spot. Kristen kept walking and waving them on, convinced it was further down the road. "Here it is. I remember this stack of small grey rocks." She started to walk quickly through the woods with her parents close behind until she came to a stand of majestic white pines, instantly feeling some relief from the sweltering day. Her parents entered the quiet area, observing the scenery, hoping it would lead them to Jule. "Look! There's his backpack," Mom said, pointing toward a fallen ash tree. Kristen ran over to it and held up a plastic bag containing a few sunflower seeds. "He's been feeding the chickadees." Mom and Dad both breathed a sigh of relief figuring he was probably fishing down by the river. This time, Dad led the way toward the river listening for its soothing melody. The water level was lower now, so they were almost upon it before they heard the river's coaxing song. They moved quickly to the place where Dad and Jule had fished on his birthday. Dad looked over by the poplar

Jule's Story

tree near the rocks they had sat on to eat lunch. "There's the Shakespeare Ugly Stik we gave him for his birthday!" he said, pointing toward it.

"But where's Jule?" Mom said, as the knot in her stomach tightened. They moved together, like there was a rope enveloping them, toward the tree as if it held some secret as to where he was. Dad picked up the rod while Kristen circled the tree.

"Here's another Shakespeare Ugly Stik leaning on the other side of it."

The three of them stood silently staring at the rods. After careful examination, Dad concluded they were identical.

"Wait a minute," Mom said. "What did Jule say last night?" She wished she had paid more attention to his story, as her heart began pounding in her chest.

"Something about the hand grip of the one Albert gave him coming off?" Kristen said, trying to turn it. "This end doesn't come off," she said, standing it back against the tree, concluding it was just another part of Jule's story.

"This one does!" Dad said, easily removing the hand grip with a loud pop. Kristen being her nosy self quickly stepped closer to him and tried to look in first. "Wow! Look at this," Dad said, peering into the hand grip. "It's just as Jule described it last night. It's like looking into a kaleidoscope, only much more colourful and vibrant!"

"Surrounding the mark of Sedna," Mom said, looking over his shoulder at the 'J' shape, as panic overwhelmed her.

He gave the hand grip to Kristen who for once stood speechless and totally mesmerized by what she saw.

"Okay. Let's be rational," he said trying to make sense of all this. "We have two rods."

"That definitely aren't identical," Kristen interjected, still staring wide-eyed into the hand grip.

"And a story about a twin named Albert that Jule told us last night around the bonfire," he continued.

"You don't suppose that Jule would have been taken ..." Mom couldn't finish the sentence, as tears welled up in her eyes.

"Don't even think that," Dad said, running his hands through his hair trying not to panic. He had to be brave for the girls. "He's got to be around here somewhere. Jule! Jule!" They stood quietly waiting for an answer.

"He's gone away with his twin!" Mom said, hysterically.

"He wouldn't do that!" Dad said angrily, pacing back and forth beside the water.

As if in a trance, Kristen began walking quickly down the river trying to find Jule. She was not as convinced as her mom that he had taken off with his so-called twin, Albert. *When I get my hands on Jule, I'm going to ring his stupid little neck ...* she stopped and stared down at the ground. "Mom, Dad. Come quick!" she yelled, not taking her eyes off the ground. "Look at this," she said, pointing down toward a large bare spot a few metres from the river. Her parents stared dumbfounded at the fresh imprint of a large 'J' surrounded by the most vibrant colours that looked more like an artist's painting than a brilliant mark in the sand.

"The mark of Sedna!" Mom gasped.

"It's also the same fishhook shape that the steelhead was mounted on that day Jule brought the fish home," Dad said, remembering how adamant he had been. "He told me his twin had whittled it and I didn't believe him."

"You don't suppose ... I can't even say it," Mom said, placing her hand over her mouth. "What if his twin took him away to Sedna?" she asked, as tears filled her eyes.

"Jule wouldn't go!" Dad said, trying to hold back his emotions.

Jule's Story

"Then where is he?" Kristen sighed, looking up toward the sky.

Jule sat tightly strapped in a blazing orange coloured seat situated in the center of the spacecraft. He quickly discovered that looks could be deceiving, as the multi-coloured interior was larger than the great room back home. Also, from this position he could see every detail of its colourful interior, which just happened to be identical to the inside of the handgrip of the Shakespeare Ugly Stik Albert had given him. He had never seen so many shades of pink, red, green, blue, yellow, orange and brown. Even black and white shades were variable. He had assumed a space suit with its own oxygen would be mandatory, but not on flights in spacecrafts from Sedna. On the contrary, the air was very fresh and the temperature was controlled for maximum comfort.

Jule was still in shock. Everything happened so quickly once he reluctantly released the fish and agreed to accompany Albert back to Sedna. After he convinced Jule that his family wouldn't miss him, and that it would only be a short trip, Albert asked him to follow him back to where they left the fishing rods. Halfway there, Albert stopped, like he was listening for something. Then he pointed to a bare patch of ground near the river.

Jule had no sooner asked why they had stopped when a shiny pewter-coloured spacecraft appeared before them. It was as tall as them, with the distinct fishhook or 'J' mark of Sedna on its side, again surrounded by glowing colours too numerous to name. Jule had walked around it and started to laugh. There were no windows and the diameter of the round, not quite 150 centimeters high tube, could not have been any more than 65 centimeters around. Before he had a chance to ask Albert if this was his preferred mode of transportation, Albert had instructed him to place his right hand on top of his twin's left, to which he complied. Next thing Jule knew, he was sitting in the seat he presently occupied, and on his way to Sedna.

"I want to show you something?" Albert said, pressing a bright pink and maroon button on the control panel. Before Jule could ask what, in a split second his seat was positioned beside a rectangular window no larger than that of a jet. There had been no windows when he walked around the spacecraft back on Earth and he wondered once again how Albert made one appear.

"Look to your left," Albert said, adjusting the magnification of the glass with the turn of a florescent, deep mauve knob.

"It's my mom and dad! And Kristen! They're standing by the river where we left the Shakespeare Ugly Stiks." He wondered if they had remembered what he had told them last night about the difference between the two rods. What was totally mind boggling was they were already billions of kilometers away, and gazing out the window it looked as if they were only a few metres away. Jule could see his mother was crying. And his father was rubbing his forehead like he always does when he's not sure what to do. And Kristen was staring up into the sky, sitting on the rock he liked to sit on when he fished. Suddenly, he felt squeamish and uneasy. Maybe this trip to Sedna wasn't a good idea after all. He watched his father hug his mother and sister, but only for a moment. Albert pushed the pink and maroon button, returning him back to the center of the spaceship.

Jule sat quietly and watched Albert man the spacecraft, when suddenly it dawned on him what Albert had been up to by giving him the Shakespeare Ugly Stik. He knew all along there was no way Jule's family would believe his stories last night, especially the one about an invisible twin. Albert had successfully pitted him against his family. So much so, he decided to leave the familiarity of home and accompany Albert to somewhere completely unknown. Jule sunk lower in his seat trying to hold back his tears as he realized what he had done, and that he may never see his family again. He stared at Albert flicking on switches and pulling at the colourful knobs. The knot in his stomach tightened. Jule wished he had never laid eyes on his twin from Sedna.

Albert looked over his shoulder. "By the looks on your family's faces, they finally believe your story. The sad part is, they should have believed you right from the beginning. Like your dad said 'the truth comes out in the end'."

Jule closed his eyes and thought about his family standing by the river, and when he opened them once again, they had landed safely on Sedna, the tenth planet.

Coming Soon from Pine Lake Books

Bellus Terra
by Tammy Woodrow

Bellus Terra is a magical place filled with flowers and stones, moss and toadstools, and many things hidden within. To a human's eye this would look like nothing more than a garden with normal garden things growing there, because that's what *they* want it to be.

"*They*" are the tiny creatures that keep this place alive with work and magic and hope for always.

"*They*" are the fairies, the pixies, the insects, and animals that work hand in hand to keep flowers blooming and seeds sprouting, to keep grasses growing and plants alive.

This is what they do!

This is why they are!

The Keepers, the Helpers, the Ones that give life to the garden!

From high into the sky where the canopy of a large beautiful maple tree opens and down its thick base where plants grow in unison, this place is known to these creatures as Bellus Terra. It is mostly a quiet part of the garden where usually the passing of a dog or a cat is more common than a person. However, there are some days when a young child would find itself at the base of that tree looking so closely for some sign of life. Hoping that they would be the first to spot a fairy or two dancing among the flowers, if not fairies then perhaps a butterfly or a praying mantis might be awesome to see. Possibly to catch a dragonfly and then to let it go again! This is a wish that almost all children have had, at least a time or two! If they only knew about the Terrafays, the

Serofays and the faylings of the garden 'Bellus Terra' they would undoubtedly visit more often.

Come take a closer look at their world!

Coming August 2010

Lorah's Promise
By Ann Harris

Banks of angry black storm clouds gathered overhead. The air was stifling hot. Not a bird sang; not a frog croaked. The only sound breaking the eerie silence was the creaking of the nine wagons as they bounced over the stony trail leading to the fast running river. Looking skyward, Lorah listened to the rumblings of thunder that sounded like a never-ending drum roll. She wiped the damp hair away from her hot, sticky forehead. "I be thinking a fierce storm is brewing, Da."

"Aye lass, 'tis a terrible angry looking sky," replied her father. "I'm thinking we'd best be stopping a while by those trees over yonder." He pointed to a thicket of trees across the river. Turning around and raising his arm, he signalled to the wagons full of immigrant families to follow him toward the trees. Slapping the leather lines, he urged Caleb, the ox, towards the sandy slope leading into the river.

Lorah felt a chilling as the hot wind became cool and large raindrops began falling. A sudden cloudburst drenched everything it touched. In seconds, the thin dress she was wearing became saturated, clinging to her body like a second skin. The rain ran in rivulets off her da's broad brimmed hat, as he struggled to hold onto the slippery lines. Caleb twisted his muscular neck, and lowered his head in an effort to avoid the driving rain.

The ox hesitated on the edge of the fast moving water. Slapping the lines over his rump, Lorah's da urged him forward. "Yah Caleb, go!" The obedient ox splashed into the water, stumbling on the slippery rocks. His muscles strained as he leaned into the yoke and pulled hard against the strong current. "Yah Caleb!" The reins once more slapped across his rump. The wagon swayed and rolled precariously as its wheels bumped over the rocks, water spraying up its' sides.

"'Tis getting deeper, Da," said Lorah, her hands gripping the side of the seat. She looked nervously at the rapidly moving water.

"Aye lass, we must be quick and get all the wagons safely across." He turned and yelled to the following wagons, "Close up now, we must hurry."

Sitting behind Lorah were her two sisters Alice and Mary, her brother James, and their mam Annie. Jostled around by the bouncing, they were now huddling together and trying to keep warm and dry as the rain blew into the open ended, covered wagon. The first flashes of lightning lit up the darkened sky. Alice squeezed her eyes tightly closed and clamped her hands over her ears as a loud clap of thunder followed.

When the wagons reached the far side of the river, the oxen, sensing shelter, needed no encouragement as they pulled the wagons at a faster pace towards the trees. The thick growth of towering cedars and hemlocks was a welcome refuge from the storm for the group of tired and wet travelers. Lightning flashed and thunder crashed overhead as each wagon pulled under the welcoming branches of the trees and out of the torrential rain.

"Come, James," said his da, as he stepped down from the wagon. "Let's help the other men tend the oxen."

"Da, where are the Quinlans?" asked Lorah. Shielding her eyes against the biting rain, she looked back towards the river. "There be only eight wagons here in the trees."

"Are you sure Lorah?"

"Aye. I went looking for Catherine, and their wagon isn't with the others. 'Tis worried I be, for she's still not recovered properly from the fever she caught on the ship."

"Hush, lass. Don't fret. James and I will away and find them. Go help yer mam and we'll be back soon."

Coming September 2010